IN HIS IMAGE - HEROES OF MY MIND

JAMES SMITH

Dear Reader,

Before we dive into this devotional, I want to take a moment to acknowledge the beautiful journey you're on. Whether you're reading this at the start of your day, in the midst of a difficult season, or simply seeking a moment of peace, I pray that these words resonate deeply with your heart. The message you're about to read is one of compassion, grace, and love—the kind of love that doesn't come with conditions, but flows freely from the heart of God. My hope is that, as you reflect on these thoughts, you will be encouraged to see yourself and others through the eyes of empathy, and that you will be inspired to extend grace in ways that transform both you and the world around you.

Now, with an open heart, let's dive into a message about giving grace for grace's sake.

Devotional: Empathy and Love – Giving Grace for Grace's Sake

Imagine walking through a bustling city street, surrounded by strangers who brush past you without a second thought. It's easy to feel invisible, as if your struggles and pain are unnoticed in the sea of people. Perhaps you've been hurt by others, misunderstood, or cast aside by a world that values success over compassion. And in those moments, it's easy to think that your worth is tied to the opinions of others, to the judgments of those who don't see the fullness of your story.

We live in a world that constantly invites us to judge and compare. We look at others and see their victories, their appearances, their carefully curated lives. But we also see our own inadequacies, our mistakes, our flaws—and the weight of comparison can be crushing. In these moments, it's tempting to react with anger or resentment, feeling that the world owes us something or that others should meet our expectations.

*But Jesus offers us a different path, one that cuts through the noise of comparison and judgment. He invites us to **see through His eyes**—eyes that are filled with empathy and love, not condemnation.*

Reflect on the story of the Good Samaritan in Luke 10:25-37. A man, beaten and left for dead on the roadside, is passed by two people—a priest and a Levite—who make no effort to help. To them, he's not a fellow human in need; he's an inconvenience, someone unworthy of their attention. They may have had reasons—maybe they were in a hurry, or maybe they feared becoming involved—but whatever their motives, they chose to walk on without offering assistance.

*Then, a Samaritan comes along. **A Samaritan**—someone considered an outsider, someone viewed with disdain by the Jews of the time. But unlike the others, he sees the man with compassion. He doesn't judge him for his situation or ask how he got there. He simply responds with love, offering his own resources and time to care for the wounded man.*

Through this story, Jesus imparts a powerful lesson about grace. He reveals that love isn't about who has earned it or who meets our standards of "deserving." It's about seeing others through the eyes of empathy, with God's heart, and choosing to respond with love, no matter their background, status, or appearance.

Grace for Grace's Sake

In a world that judges, compares, and attaches conditions to love, Jesus calls us to a completely different path. He urges us to offer grace—not because someone has earned it or "deserves" it—but simply because grace is a gift. Just as God has freely and unconditionally extended His grace to us, He calls us to give grace for grace's own sake.

This doesn't mean we ignore the pain or the wrongs of the world; it means we choose to respond to others with empathy, not out of a sense of obligation, but out of the same love that God has poured into us. ***We love because we have been loved. We show grace because we have received grace.***

Jesus shows us that love is not about the surface—it's about seeing the person underneath, acknowledging their humanity, and extending compassion. ***Empathy isn't just understanding someone's pain, but also understanding that they are worthy of grace, just as we are.***

Reflection:

- ***When you feel judged or compared to others, how does it impact your ability to love and show grace?*** *How can you shift your perspective to focus on what you can give rather than what you lack?*

- ***Think of someone in your life who may not seem deserving of grace.*** *What would it look like to offer them love and empathy, as Jesus did for the Good Samaritan?*

- ***Grace is a choice****—it's not something we wait to feel, but something we choose to give. How can you choose to extend grace today, regardless of whether someone "deserves" it?*

Closing Prayer:

Father, thank You for the grace You have poured into my life. You loved me before I was born, and You continue to love me despite my flaws. Help me to see others with Your eyes—eyes filled with compassion, empathy, and love. Teach me to extend grace to those around me, not because they've earned it, but because I have received Your grace. When I am tempted to judge or compare, remind me of the love You showed me through the cross, and help me to love others in the same way. In Jesus' name, Amen.

With that in mind, I also want to invite you into another journey I've created: In His Image: Heroes of My Mind—a fictional psychological thriller that I hope will captivate and challenge your heart and mind in its own unique way. I truly hope you enjoy the adventure and the insights it brings.

ABOUT THE AUTHOR

James Smith (Pen Name: Sophia Weiss)

James Smith, known by his **pen name** *Sophia Weiss*, is the author of several works that bridge the realms of philosophy and storytelling. His first work of fiction, ***The Journal of Surrender***, introduced readers to a deeply introspective journey that intertwined ancient wisdom with personal transformation. With his latest novel, ***In His Image - Heroes of My Mind***, James marks the second official chapter of his literary fiction career, where philosophy, power, and human complexity come together in a gripping psychological thriller.

Though known for his non-fiction works—***Ancient Greek Mythology and Its Influence on Western Civilization***, ***Stoic Lessons for a Better Life: Virtues to Guide My Soul***, and ***The Art of Entertaining Ideas: The Halls of Greek Philosophers***—James has long explored the intersection of ancient philosophy and contemporary life. His non-fiction books reflect his passion for classical studies and how they shape modern understanding of self and society. With his novels, James brings that same deep intellectual exploration into narrative form, where introspection meets high-stakes storytelling.

A lifelong student of philosophy and classical thought, James's writing often reflects his admiration for ancient wisdom, but with a twist: he explores how these timeless teachings continue to impact our complex, modern lives. ***In***

His Image - Heroes of My Mind delves into the psyche of Katya Vasilieva, a woman whose dark vision of ultimate power challenges everything society holds dear. Blurring the lines between reality and madness, this book examines themes of control, ambition, and the dangerous pursuit of godhood.

James believes that, just like philosophy, fiction holds the power to shape minds, ignite introspection, and drive transformation. With *In His Image*, he challenges readers to confront the true nature of power, morality, and the extremes one might go to in their pursuit of control. His aim is not only to entertain, but to provoke deep reflection on the motivations, choices, and forces that shape their own lives and the world around them.

Born and raised in Salem, Oregon, James remains deeply immersed in the study of philosophy and the human condition. Drawing from a diverse range of philosophical traditions, he creates works that delve into the challenge of living authentically in a world rife with complexity, doubt, and self-deception. Whether through fiction or non-fiction, his writing urges readers to examine the very core of their beliefs, understand what they truly stand for, and question their assumptions about both the world and themselves.

PROLOGUE

"She who seeks the throne with hands stained by ambition will never sit in peace. Power granted by force is no gift—it is a weight, a chain, and a silent killer. Those who believe they can bend the world to their will shall find themselves bent beneath it. Her end will not be at the hands of others, nor by the weight of a blade—but by the burden of her own soul. And when she falls, it will be as those who climbed too high, their gaze set on the heavens, never seeing the ground slip from beneath them."

1

THE GIRL IN THE ASYLUM

Russia, Early 2000s

Ekaterina Vasilieva stood in the center of the sterile, white room, motionless, her dark eyes fixed on the cold metal bars of the window. Beyond them, the world was nothing but a blur of gray, a stark contrast to the suffocating silence inside the psychiatric ward. The peeling walls and flickering fluorescent lights made it feel more like a prison than a place of healing. And yet, it was here, in this sterile cell, that she had begun to understand her own power.

At fourteen, they had already labeled her broken—her mind shattered by the death of her younger brother, Donovan. The doctors whispered about delusions, paranoia, and guilt—twisting her thoughts into a labyrinth of madness. But they were wrong.

The truth was far simpler.

She wasn't crazy. She was powerful.

The staff didn't understand her. Their medications barely dulled the sharp edges of her mind, and none of their treatments could touch the most important part of her—

her visions, the voices, the knowledge that had unfolded like a secret map in her mind. Donovan's death hadn't been an accident. He had been her path, her sacrifice. And his soul? It was hers now.

"They'll see," she whispered to herself, her voice soft but sure. "They'll all see."

The sharp, purposeful footsteps down the hall snapped her out of her reverie. Dr. Anatov was coming for his daily checkup. He was predictable—routine. He would ask her the same questions, look at her with that false pity, as if she were fragile, broken. But he was wrong. The time for games was over. She knew exactly what was coming.

The door creaked open, and Dr. Anatov entered, his white lab coat hanging loosely on his narrow frame. He wore a practiced look of concern—the kind that doctors put on when they felt they had to care but didn't really want to.

"Ekaterina," he said, his voice gentle but firm. "How are we feeling today?"

She didn't answer immediately, letting the silence stretch between them. Her eyes locked onto his, cold, calculating, and unreadable. She tapped her fingers rhythmically on the armrest of her chair, her lips curling just slightly, a flicker of something darker behind her gaze.

"You know why I'm here," Dr. Anatov continued, settling into the chair across from her. His eyes flicked to the notes in front of him—standard questions, standard answers. Nothing new. "Do you still believe Donovan speaks to you?"

Katya tilted her head slightly, her long hair cascading over one shoulder, obscuring part of her face. She considered his question for a moment before speaking, her voice soft, but chilling.

"Donovan has never left me," she said, her words laden

with an undeniable certainty. "He's here, in everything I do. I don't need to believe in him... he's real."

The silence thickened. She didn't speak of him as a memory, but as a presence, as though he were standing beside her, guiding her every thought and action. Dr. Anatov's eyes shifted nervously. He cleared his throat, trying to regain control.

"Ekaterina, you understand," he began, "we need to address these delusions. The trauma from losing your brother—"

"No," she interrupted sharply, her voice rising, slicing through the air. "You don't understand. You don't understand what it means to *control* a soul, to hold it in your hand like a precious thing. You think this is a sickness, but it's not. It's the truth."

Dr. Anatov blinked, taken aback by the ferocity in her voice. He scribbled something down on his notepad, but his mind raced. He had seen patients like her before—lost in their own minds, their perception of reality fractured. But there was something about Ekaterina that unsettled him. Something *different*.

"You have to realize," he said carefully, trying to stay calm, "what you're saying—what you believe—it's not real, Ekaterina. The world doesn't work that way. You can't control life and death like that. It's... impossible."

Katya leaned forward, her eyes locking onto his with unnerving intensity. Her lips quirked into the faintest of smiles.

"Impossible?" she repeated softly, almost amused. "That's what they said about Hitler. That's what they said about Stalin. And yet... here we are."

Her words hung in the air, chilling the room. She didn't wait for his response. Instead, her thoughts began to shift again, away from the doctor, away from the sterile room. The walls seemed to fade as she retreated into the labyrinth of her mind.

Five laws, she thought, her fingers absently tapping on the table in front of her. They weren't just abstract ideas—they were a blueprint, a code that had been laid out for her. A map to ultimate power.

The First Law: Master Death

He who controls life and death controls the soul of the masses.

Death was the key to everything. People feared it—feared the end of their fragile existence—and that fear could be molded, twisted, and used to control them. Not through the flash of a bullet or the suddenness of a blade, but through something more insidious. The threat of death, lurking at the edges of every moment, ready to consume anyone at any time. That was where power lay.

The Second Law: Eliminate the Expendable

The weak, the criminal, the unworthy—these are the tools that must be discarded. Only then can the strong inherit the earth.

The unworthy had to be eradicated. Donovan's death had been the first step—necessary, painful, but it had paved the way. In this place, she would begin to cleanse. Those who served no purpose, those who dragged the system down, had to go. Only the strong, the loyal, the pure would remain to serve the vision.

.   .   .

The Third Law: Control the Narrative

Those who control the past control the future. A society without history is a society without direction.

History was malleable, like clay. She could twist it, reshape it, until it suited her needs. The truth of Donovan's death—her own story—was in her hands now. She would write it. They would believe it. No one would ever know the real story.

The Fourth Law: Weaponize Fear

Fear is the most powerful tool for uniting the people under your will. When they fear you, they will obey.

Fear was sharper than any knife, more binding than any chain. She would make them fear her. Fear of what she might do. Fear of her growing power. Fear of death itself. And when they feared her, they would follow her. They would bend.

The Fifth Law: Eliminate Competition

Power is like a garden; pull out the weeds before they have the chance to grow.

Her breath slowed. Dr. Anatov, the nurses—they were obstacles, weeds. They would be removed. Opposition, whether overt or subtle, had no place in her world. They would fall one by one, until nothing stood in her way. Only then could her reign truly begin.

. . .

Her thoughts solidified like ice. The five laws were not just a theory. They were the truth. They had been proven by those who came before her—the dictators, the conquerors. They hadn't achieved immortality by their actions alone. No, they had mastered the game of life and death. And now, so would she.

Her heart beat in rhythm with her thoughts, each law a step closer to something greater. Something eternal.

"They'll see," she whispered, her voice cold and unshakable. "They'll all see."

Katya could almost feel Donovan's presence again, urging her forward, whispering in her ear. She wasn't like the others. *She understood.* They never would.

As Dr. Anatov furrowed his brow, his mind struggling to understand her, the door suddenly swung open. A nurse entered, disrupting the moment. Katya's gaze flickered with irritation, but she didn't move. She didn't need to. She had already won this small battle. She would win them all.

As the nurse helped with paperwork, Katya closed her eyes, breathing deeply. Donovan's voice was clearer than ever, and this time, she could almost feel him—just out of reach.

Her time was coming.

And soon, the world would understand.

2

RELEASE AND NEW IDENTITY

Russia, Late 2000s

Ekaterina Vasilieva stood in the sterile office of the psychiatric asylum's head administrator, her back straight, her gaze unwavering. The walls, painted a dull, clinical white, seemed to close in around her, but she didn't flinch. The cold air in the room was palpable, oppressive, like a thick, invisible weight pressing down on her chest. It had always been this way—the chilling, antiseptic atmosphere of the asylum—but today it felt different. Heavier. As if the gravity of everything she had endured, everything she had lost, had finally caught up to her. But Ekaterina wasn't concerned with the cold or the suffocating silence.

She was focused on the moment she had been waiting for. The moment when they would open the door, let her out, and leave her to her own devices. She had earned this. This was her victory.

Three years. Three long, agonizing years locked away behind the walls of this place, a place filled with the mentally broken, the lost, and the hopeless. She had been trapped in the world of their delusions, their fears, their endless questions. But that was the old Ekaterina—the one who had once believed she was broken, who had believed that perhaps the doctors, with their sharp eyes and even sharper needles, knew better than she did. They had convinced her, for a while, that her beliefs were nothing more than the fantasies of a confused, grieving child.

But that Ekaterina was gone. Buried. She had shed her old identity like a skin too tight, too suffocating. The girl who had once been known as Ekaterina Nikolayevna Vasilieva, who had been the fragile daughter of a prominent Russian family, who had believed in the possibility of redemption—she was no more. She was buried beneath a new identity now, a new vision of the future. And the future, Ekaterina knew, was her own to shape.

She let her mind drift back for just a moment. In the beginning, when she had first arrived at the asylum, she had questioned everything. The doctors, the nurses, the other patients who whispered in the dark about their "demons." She had even wondered if she, too, had a demon living inside her. The questions about her brother's death haunted her in the beginning—questions she could never quite get an answer to. Was it an accident? Or was it something worse? Something darker? And how could she, a mere child, have been the one to cause it?

But every time she'd tried to ask, every time she'd voiced her confusion, the doctors had shut her down. "Delusion," they'd said, and "paranoia." They had diagnosed her with psychotic episodes, labeled her a victim of her own mind. Her obsession with Donovan's death, her belief that his spirit still spoke to her, had all been symptoms of a fractured mind, they claimed. They didn't understand. They couldn't. How could they? To them, the answer was always the same: it was just delusion.

Ekaterina had been trapped in a cage of their making. But no longer. She had learned to play the game. To give them what they wanted. Her silence. Her compliance. She had been a model patient, a docile little girl, just the way they liked it. They thought she was sick, they thought she was lost. But in truth, she was the one who had been playing them.

Her fingers tightened ever so slightly as she forced her thoughts back to the present. The administrator's office. The sound of paper shuffling. The carefully controlled voices of the doctors who believed they had unraveled her. They were wrong. They thought they had found the broken pieces of Ekaterina. But she wasn't broken. She was reborn.

Dr. Anatov, the lead psychiatrist, sat across from her, nervously tapping his pen against the desk. His brow furrowed in that familiar, clinical way. He was a man who had spent hours poring over her case, dissecting the records, charting the ebb and flow of her moods. He had thought he understood her, thought he had cracked the code. He didn't.

"Ekaterina," he began, his voice soft but authoritative, "we believe you're ready to leave now. Your treatment has been... well, it's been significant. You've made considerable progress." He cleared his throat, his eyes flicking to the papers in front of him. "We believe that with continued outpatient care, you will be able to transition back into normal life."

Outpatient care. The words felt like a mockery, like a faint echo of a past that no longer held any meaning for her. She didn't need their follow-up care. She didn't need anything from them. They had failed to see the depths of her mind, the intricate web of ideas she had constructed while they doped her with their medication and their talk therapy. She had fed them just enough to stay in their good graces, enough to bide her time until she was strong enough to leave.

The faintest smile curled at the corners of Ekaterina's lips as she met Dr. Anatov's gaze. It was a smile that didn't quite reach her eyes, one that held the coldness of a predator sizing up its prey.

"Of course, Doctor," she replied smoothly, her voice a carefully cultivated sweetness. "I understand."

He nodded, more to himself than to her, clearly satisfied that she was adhering to the script he had written. He hadn't noticed the subtle shift in her demeanor, the way her eyes darkened as she spoke. He was blind to it, as they all had been. The years she had spent inside these walls, trapped in their cages of misunderstanding, had forged her into something far more dangerous than they could comprehend.

She stood slowly, her movements precise, elegant. There was no hesitation in her step as she made her way toward the door, every inch of her body radiating a calm, controlled confidence. Ekaterina wasn't the same girl who had been ushered in here three years ago—wide-eyed, confused, and desperate for answers. She had become something else entirely.

Her hand rested on the doorknob, but before she stepped through, she turned back to Dr. Anatov. He was still staring at his papers, oblivious to the shift that had occurred.

"Thank you for everything, Doctor," she said, her voice like ice. But the words were empty, hollow. Thank you for nothing.

With a final, controlled breath, she pushed the door open and stepped out of the sterile office, the cold hallway stretching before her. The door clicked shut behind her, the sound echoing through the empty halls—sharp, final, like the sound of a coffin closing.

Her new life awaited.

The New Identity

Three days later, Ekaterina stood before the full-length mirror in a tiny, sparsely furnished apartment. The reflection that stared back at her was a stark contrast to the girl who had walked out of the psychiatric asylum. Her eyes—dark, calculating—held something that bordered on satisfaction, but beneath it, there was something colder, something darker that had always been there, just waiting to emerge.

She wasn't Ekaterina Nikolayevna Vasilieva anymore. That girl was dead. The girl who had once been broken, confused, lost in a haze of grief and delusion, was no more. She had erased her, buried her deep beneath layers of carefully crafted falsehoods. The woman staring back from the mirror wasn't a victim of circumstance. She was a force, a shadow, poised to rise.

Her hair—once the pale, almost golden shade of her youth—was now dark, sleek, and glossy. A perfect match for her new life, her new persona. A careful touch of dark brown dye had transformed her, just as everything else about her had been carefully designed. Her name, her history, her identity had all been altered with precision.

Katya Vasilieva. It was a simple name, unremarkable. But it was her shield, her armor. It was the mask she would wear for the rest of her life.

She ran a hand through her newly dyed hair, savoring the feel of its weight, the way it framed her face, how it added to the sense of rebirth. She wasn't the fragile, emotionally torn child she had once been. The girl who had cried herself to sleep in a cold, sterile room, haunted by the ghost of her brother.

Katya Vasilieva was stronger. Smarter. Calculated.

Her reflection didn't show the scars—the invisible scars, the ones that cut deeper than any blade ever could. Those were hidden beneath her well-practiced mask of charm and brilliance. The world would see her as nothing more than an idealistic, highly intelligent young woman, full of potential and ambition.

She had already done the work to ensure no one would look too closely. The passport. The forged documents. The clean slate she had created in place of her past. It had all been meticulously crafted, and in the eyes of the authorities, Ekaterina Vasilieva was just a ghost—a dead name buried beneath layers of bureaucracy and falsehood.

The walls of her new apartment were bare, like the life she was about to build. Nothing in the room would stand out. No trophies or mementos to draw attention. Nothing flashy. It was a calculated choice.

But in the back of the closet, tucked away behind a false panel in the wall, was a secret she could never let go. There, hidden from prying eyes, was a single photograph—a well-worn picture of her brother Donovan. The boy who had died under her hand. The boy she had sacrificed. His soul, now her possession.

The photograph was a token of the past, a reminder of the price she had paid for her power. But it was also a symbol of her future, of the control she now held over life and death. And the world would never know the truth.

Katya sat down at the small desk in the corner of the room. The apartment might have been plain, but it was hers. Every item in it had been chosen with care and intention. It was a reflection of the person she had become—deliberate, meticulous, and in control.

The laptop in front of her hummed to life, the screen flickering for a moment before it stabilized. It had been her tool of choice during her years in the asylum. During her time in isolation, she had learned to code, to hack, to infiltrate systems that were never meant for people like her. It had been a secret obsession, one that she had nurtured in silence. The doctors had never suspected. They had thought her passive, a quiet student of the world, someone who only read books and solved puzzles. But Ekaterina—now Katya—had always been thinking ahead, calculating. And now it was time to make her move.

She glanced at the acceptance letter from the American university. She would study biology, history, philosophy—subjects that would provide the foundation for her new ambitions. She had always been a prodigy, but now she had a purpose. She wasn't studying these subjects for knowledge alone; she was studying them to learn how to manipulate life and death, to understand how to **control it.**

Stalin. Hitler. Ivan the Terrible. These were the figures she admired, the ones who had wielded power over death itself. They had left their marks on history, not just through their cruelty, but by taking lives, by dictating who lived and who died. She had read about them for years, studied their tactics, their ruthlessness. They were more than dictators to her. They were gods.

And she would become one.

Her fingers hovered over the keyboard, opening the documents she had prepared for the next phase. The U.S.

Department of Corrections' food distribution system was vulnerable. She had already infiltrated parts of it, gathering data on how food was distributed to the country's most dangerous criminals. She didn't want to act too quickly, though. Not yet. First, she needed to settle in. Lay the groundwork.

The poison she planned to use—specially crafted, slow-acting—was already in her mind. She would perfect it over time, ensure it could bypass all the usual safety measures. It would be a weapon no one saw coming. A subtle, silent execution that could kill thousands without anyone realizing until it was too late.

But all of that would come later. The foundation had to be laid first. She couldn't act in haste. She had learned that in the asylum. Patience. Time. Precision.

Katya closed her laptop with a soft click. She stood up and walked to the window, looking out at the city stretching before her. The sky was overcast, the faint gray light filtering through the clouds, but there was something almost poetic about the scene. This was her canvas.

With each step she took, her plan would unfold. The future, her future, was a thing of shadows and silence. Every move she made would be calculated, deliberate, and unnoticed until it was too late for anyone to stop her.

She turned from the window and glanced once more at the mirror. The woman who looked back at her was Katya Vasilieva—young, bright, and full of promise. But beneath the surface, lurking in the depths, was the true force that would reshape everything.

The monster was alive.

Adoption and Reinvention

A few weeks later, Katya was welcomed into the home of the Harrison family—an affluent American couple with a warm heart and an unyielding desire to help others. They had volunteered to take in exchange students, offering young minds from all over the world a chance to thrive in the United States. The Harrisons were kind, loving, and blissfully unaware of the storm they had unknowingly invited into their home.

Katya played her role to perfection. She had become the ideal daughter—polite, intelligent, grateful—never stepping out of line. To the Harrisons, she was everything they had hoped for in a foreign exchange student, their pride and joy. They showered her with affection, taking her to family gatherings and ensuring she felt welcomed and loved.

But Katya wasn't just playing a part. She had already begun to manipulate the environment, setting the stage for what came next. With the Harrisons' wealth, connections, and their established place in society, she now had the perfect platform to launch her next move. She didn't need much from them—just enough to slip under the radar. The warmth of their home, the illusion of family, gave her the perfect cover. No one would suspect that the quiet, sweet girl they had welcomed into their lives was anything but innocent.

Her real work had already begun. She used her time wisely, cultivating an image of the ideal student while quietly observing, absorbing the resources she needed. Her academic background—carefully curated in Russia— opened doors to elite universities. But more importantly, it gave her the ability to execute her next deadly steps without drawing suspicion. The world was hers for the taking, and she would not stop until it bowed to her.

As she lay in her darkened bedroom at night, the silence enveloping her like a cloak, Donovan's voice still whispered in her ear. *"You're almost there, Katya. It's time. They'll all kneel before you."*

Her mind burned with ambition. The Harrisons had given her a new name, a fresh start, and the illusion of a life she would never truly claim. But that was all it was—an illusion. In the shadows of their perfect world, Katya Vasilieva was already building something far greater.

The world would soon be hers to control. And when it did, no one—least of all the Harrisons—would ever know what she had done to get there.

3
THE FOREIGN EXCHANGE PROGRAM

New York City, USA, Early 2010s

Katya's first steps onto American soil were almost deliberate, the way a predator steps into its territory—calculated and aware. The rush of people around her, the cacophony of voices and honking cars, the bright chaos of New York City—it all felt so new, yet so... familiar. She had been preparing for this for years.

Katya had been accepted into the prestigious exchange program at Columbia University, something she'd orchestrated with her characteristic precision. Her academic credentials were impeccable—multiple degrees in philosophy, biology, and history, all forged from her life in Russia under her previous identity. She had carefully manipulated every step of the process, pulling strings, controlling the narrative, shaping herself into someone the Americans would never suspect.

Her adoptive parents, the Harrisons, were thrilled. Their excitement was palpable as they spoke about her future, introducing her to the wonders of American life. But Katya only nodded and smiled. Their enthusiasm was touching in a way, but it was insignificant. They were nothing more than pawns in her grand game.

"Katya, I'm so glad we're able to have you here," Mrs. Harrison said, her voice warm as they drove into the heart of Manhattan. "We're just so proud of everything you've accomplished. You're going to do so well here."

Katya glanced out the window, her eyes flashing with something sharp. The city was magnificent, overwhelming even, but she had bigger plans than sightseeing or settling into an easy routine. She wasn't here to get a degree. She was here to execute her vision-the five laws of power.

"Yes, I'm looking forward to it," she replied, her voice soft, measured. She kept her gaze fixed on the skyline, her mind already calculating her next steps.

The first order of business was to blend in. At Columbia, Katya was just another brilliant student—intelligent, poised, and meticulous. She kept her distance from others, never letting them get too close, but always presenting herself as the ideal student. She turned in flawless assignments, participated in class discussions with ease, and quickly earned the respect of professors and peers alike.

But there was something more beneath the surface, something darker. She wasn't just studying biology or philosophy. She was studying humanity—its weaknesses, its obsessions with power and death. She'd already completed a research paper on eugenics, drawing parallels between historical figures who had manipulated life and death. Her professors were impressed, but they had no idea how personal that research was.

Katya's real education, however, was taking place in seclusion—in the quiet, hidden spaces where she could practice her true art. Hacking. Manipulating. Controlling. She spent hours perfecting her skills, diving deep into the world of code, data, and encryption. Her fingers moved effortlessly across the keyboard, breaking into systems that most people wouldn't even know existed. She was gathering information, making connections, and quietly laying the groundwork for what would come next.

At Columbia, she was just a top student. In the shadows, she was already something much more. And no one—no one—would ever see her coming.

The First Steps of Her Plan

One evening, after her classes, Katya sat alone in her sparse apartment, the soft glow of her laptop screen casting a cold light over her features. The world outside could wait—television, distractions, even the noise of New York City were meaningless. Her mind was consumed by one thing only: the next step in her grand design.

Her target? The U.S. Department of Corrections' food distribution system. A behemoth of bureaucracy, sprawling and tangled, yet overlooked by nearly everyone. But Katya was not everyone. She had already begun her infiltration. Armed with patience and precision, she'd navigated the digital labyrinth, pulling up internal files and identifying weaknesses.

The poison—her key to the entire operation—had been selected months ago. A rare, slow-acting toxin, one that would leave no trace. The beauty of it was its subtlety. Administered through food, it would be undetectable. And with each step of her meticulous plan, she was ensuring that no one could trace it back to her.

Her list of targets was already set—those who had destroyed lives, those whose actions had left scars on the world. The murderers, the rapists, the traffickers. As if offering a silent prayer to herself—and to the world—Katya whispered softly, "The Second Law: Eliminate the Expendable."

Yes, they would be the first to fall. This law would lay the groundwork for everything else to unfold. Her vision was unwavering: purge them from existence, claim their souls, and inch closer to her ascension. In her mind, this wasn't just a mission—it was destiny. A cold, calculated experiment in control. Death was not an end; it could be shaped, twisted, harnessed. And through it, she would become something more. Immortal.

Katya's fingers flew over the keys, each tap deliberate, precise. She was no mere hacker. She was a strategist, a mastermind of systems both digital and human. With every line of code, she was bending the system to her will. She was creating her own world, one where she was the judge, the jury, and the executioner. No one could stop her, and no one would ever see her coming.

As she worked, a faint, almost imperceptible smile curled at the edges of her lips. She could hear Donovan's voice in her mind, quiet but insistent—urging her forward. You're almost there. You're so close now.

Katya leaned back in her chair, eyes narrowing with satisfaction. The pieces were falling into place, and soon, her plan would unfold exactly as she had envisioned. The world would be forced to bow to her. All she had to do was strike.

The Investigative Journalist

As Katya's plan began to take form, a shadow crept closer—one she had yet to sense. Someone was starting to notice the strange, underlying patterns of her actions.

Someone who was already on her trail, though he didn't know it yet.

Étienne Lemoine, a seasoned French investigative journalist known for his relentless pursuit of the most elusive and dangerous stories, had been tracking a series of bizarre disappearances across the United States. At first, it appeared to be nothing more than random acts of violence, but Étienne's sharp mind soon saw a disturbing trend. These disappearances weren't random—they were methodical, purposeful, and terrifyingly precise.

His investigation had led him to an unsettling realization: the missing people all had one thing in common. They were incarcerated criminals, dangerous individuals who had disappeared without a trace. At first, he had thought they had escaped, or been silenced by someone with power. But as he dug deeper, he noticed a chilling connection. Each one of the missing prisoners had eaten meals provided by the same food distributor—a small, unassuming company contracted by the U.S. Department of Corrections. Étienne's instincts told him that this was no coincidence. Something was off.

His investigation was still in its infancy when Katya first came across his name. She was sitting alone in her apartment, her fingers flying across the keyboard, navigating through encrypted emails and classified government documents. It was then that an article on Étienne's investigation caught her eye. The headline was innocuous enough —*Investigative Journalist Uncovers Pattern in Missing Prisoners*—but the moment Katya read the words, her heart skipped a beat.

Étienne Lemoine was too close. This journalist was probing into the very thing she had worked so hard to conceal.

A chill ran down Katya's spine as she stared at his photo. His features were sharp, his eyes dark with the kind of exhaustion only someone who had chased truths others didn't want found could wear. He had the look of a man who didn't give up. And that was the problem. Étienne Lemoine was a threat.

But in that moment, Katya recognized something else: his weakness. He was logical, methodical—a man of patterns, of evidence, of reason. And that made him predictable. He would be easy to mislead, to manipulate. She could throw him off her trail with a few well-placed distractions. It was child's play for her.

Her fingers hovered over the keyboard as a plan began to form in her mind. She could erase every trace of her involvement from his investigation. All she had to do was create the perfect red herring. A few carefully crafted false leads, a series of misdirected clues—Étienne would follow the wrong path, chasing ghosts like all the others.

Katya smiled to herself, a cold, calculating smile. She knew exactly how to handle Étienne. He wouldn't even see her coming.

The Beginning of the Cat-and-Mouse Game

A few days later, in the dimly lit office of his apartment in Paris, Étienne sat hunched over his desk, the scattered pages of his investigation spread before him. He had been working late, tracing every lead, every pattern. The disappearances were beginning to make sense—more than just a series of isolated events, they were connected by something deeper. His mind raced as he scribbled notes, trying to piece it all together.

Just then, a new email popped into his inbox. The

subject line was unremarkable: *Prison Food Supplier – Delivery Irregularities.*

At first glance, it seemed like a throwaway tip—nothing more than a routine complaint about food delivery delays at a U.S. prison. A small discrepancy, probably nothing more than bureaucratic sloppiness. But as Étienne began to read, a feeling of unease settled in his chest. The details were too precise, the language too polished. It was as if the person behind the tip knew exactly what he was looking for —too much so.

The report mentioned irregularities in meal schedules, discrepancies in food deliveries, and a series of unexplained changes in the prison's contracted supplier. But it wasn't the content of the message that raised Étienne's suspicions —it was the tone. It was clean, almost scripted. Too perfect, too well-informed for what should have been a minor bureaucratic issue.

This was no ordinary anonymous tip. Someone was trying to lead him somewhere. Someone was deliberately steering him off course, forcing his attention to an inconsequential lead.

But who? And why?

The question gnawed at him as he sat back in his chair, his eyes narrowing. Whoever had sent this knew exactly how to manipulate him. The game had just shifted. And now, Étienne Lemoine was a player, just like everyone else.

4
THE EMERGENCE OF
THE PLAN

New York City, Late 2010s

Katya stood before the large, gleaming stainless-steel fridge in her apartment, her fingers lightly brushing the cold surface. She had spent months preparing for this moment—every decision, every calculation, every detail carefully orchestrated. This wasn't just a plan. This was her masterpiece, years in the making. And now, as she faced the culmination of all her efforts, a shiver of anticipation ran through her.

With a steady hand, she opened the fridge door, the familiar sound of the hinge creaking in the silence of the room. Inside, the shelves were neat and organized, but her eyes went immediately to one corner—the small, innocuous containers of mushrooms. To anyone else, they would appear as nothing more than a curiosity or a specialty food item, exotic and perhaps a little out of place. But to Katya, they were the key. The weapon.

The mushrooms were a rare variety—wild fungi harvested from deep in the forests of Eastern Europe, an area few would venture into. Katya had tracked down the very people who knew how to find them, paid top dollar for them, and spent years studying their properties. The toxins they contained were slow-acting, subtle in their execution. The symptoms would take hours to manifest, and by the time the victim realized something was wrong, it would be far too late.

She picked up a small container, running her thumb over the label. The mushrooms had been dried, ground, and refined to perfection. She had painstakingly extracted their venom, turning it into a deadly, colorless liquid. A clear toxin that shimmered faintly when exposed to light, almost innocent-looking. In reality, it was a precise, calculated agent of death, designed for maximum effect without leaving a trace.

Katya's eyes glinted with cold determination as she reached into the back of the fridge. Her fingers closed around several small vials, each one containing the deadly extract she had created herself. The liquid inside the vials was translucent, almost ethereal, like poison distilled to perfection. She had tested it, of course—on small animals, in secret. She was patient. Methodical. No one would ever know it was her, no one would ever understand the exact mechanics of her weapon. It was flawless. It had to be.

She unscrewed the cap of one vial, and as the liquid filled the small syringe, she watched the way it swirled, mesmerizing in its simplicity. Each dose was meticulously measured, enough to bring about the slow, agonizing paralysis of the respiratory system. The victim would struggle for breath, helpless as their own body betrayed them, suffocating them inch by inch.

Katya had infiltrated the U.S. Department of Corrections' food distribution system weeks ago. She had hacked into their network, leaving no trace of her intrusion, and replaced one of the established food suppliers with a fake, anonymous company she controlled from the shadows. Now, every meal being delivered to the prisons would carry her toxin. The prisoners—those convicted of the most heinous crimes—would unknowingly become part of her experiment.

She carefully filled the syringes, one for each shipment of food, her movements fluid and precise. Each one was sealed tightly, each one a deadly promise. The supplier was scheduled to make its next delivery in the morning. By the time the sun rose, the process would be underway. Each meal, each bite, would be a step closer to her final goal.

Her hand hovered over the syringes, pausing for a moment. Her thoughts drifted to Donovan, the brother she had sacrificed for her own power. She could hear his voice in her mind, faint but clear, a whisper from beyond the grave. *They will pay. All of them. They must pay.*

Her lips curled into a smile, but it was cold, almost feral. She wasn't just killing these men to cleanse the world of their sins. She was claiming their souls. Their deaths would serve as sacrifices in her ascension to godhood. Every life she took would strengthen her, empower her. And with each death, her vision of immortality would come closer to reality. She would reign over all. The world would bow to her, or it would burn.

Katya took a deep breath, steadying herself. The weight of what she was about to do didn't faze her. This was simply the next step. It was all part of the plan. A plan that was now unfolding perfectly, each piece falling into place with chilling precision.

She packed the syringes into a small, inconspicuous bag. The handle was soft under her fingers as she slipped it into her coat pocket, the bag a silent companion in her meticulously crafted world. The next morning, the food would be delivered. The deaths would begin.

And Katya Vasilieva—soon to be something more than human—would take the next step toward her ultimate power.

Étienne's Growing Suspicion

Étienne Lemoine leaned back in his worn office chair, rubbing his temples as he scanned the anonymous tip once again. The soft hum of the overhead light was the only sound in the room, a steady drone that did nothing to ease the tension coiling in his chest. His tired eyes darted back and forth across the email. On the surface, it seemed inconsequential—a minor report about irregularities in a prison food supplier's delivery schedule. But as he studied the details, something gnawed at him. The timing, the phrasing, the way the information had been presented—it was all too neat, too deliberate.

Whoever had sent it, Étienne was sure of one thing: they were trying to mislead him.

It wasn't the first time he'd encountered a diversion in his investigations, but this one felt different. The leads he had been chasing on the string of mysterious deaths had been strange from the beginning, but now, they were starting to feel too orchestrated. Each new clue seemed to be pushing him further off the trail, suggesting coincidences where there were none, pointing toward culprits who didn't add up. This was no longer a simple case of missing persons or random acts of violence. The more he uncovered, the more it felt like someone was playing a game with him.

He closed his laptop and ran a hand through his hair,

his mind working furiously. The missing prisoners—the ones who had turned up dead in strange circumstances—were all linked by one thing: they were violent criminals, the kind of men society wanted to forget. But what Étienne couldn't shake was the nagging feeling that this wasn't just a story about justice being served in a twisted way. It felt like something bigger was at play. This wasn't a simple case of natural justice, nor was it an act of vengeance. It was something more calculated, something deliberate.

He leaned forward, pulling out the notes he had made about the victims: the murderers, rapists, traffickers—all men whose names carried weight in their respective dark corners of the world. But the more Étienne reviewed their deaths, the less sense it all made. These were not the sort of deaths that occurred by chance. Something, or someone, was pulling the strings.

He took another sip of his cold coffee and began retracing his steps, trying to find the link between the men. The deaths, he knew, were not entirely random. There was a pattern, one that had become clearer with every passing day. He flipped through his notes—each man had been found dead under strange circumstances, often within days of receiving meals from a specific food distributor. Some had died in their cells, others had fallen ill with symptoms that no one could explain. But there was no doubt in his mind: the deaths were connected.

Étienne's phone buzzed, the sudden noise breaking his concentration. He glanced at the screen—Claire, his inside contact at the U.S. prison system. She had been a valuable source, feeding him information for months, but their communication had been discreet and sporadic. This message was short but urgent: *"I've found something that might be important. Meet me in 20 minutes at the usual place."*

His heart skipped a beat. He didn't need to ask what she had uncovered—he already knew. Claire was meticulous, cautious. If she was calling him now, it meant she had stumbled upon something major. He grabbed his coat, already plotting the fastest route to the meeting place. His instincts told him that whatever Claire had found, it was the missing piece to the puzzle. It was the lead that would connect all the dots.

The mysteries of the disappearing prisoners, the unexplained deaths, the missing link between the food supplier and the victims—Étienne was getting closer, but he could feel the pressure mounting. Whoever was behind this was smart, calculating. And now, someone was actively trying to divert his attention. But Étienne had been doing this long enough to recognize the game. He wasn't going to let himself be misled.

As he stepped out into the night, the chill air bit at his skin, but the sense of urgency in his chest kept him moving quickly. The truth, he was certain, was just out of reach. And he wasn't about to let it slip away.

The First Deaths

The next day, as the food trays were distributed to inmates in several U.S. correctional facilities, the quiet hum of daily life continued without suspicion. Prisoners sat at their tables, shuffling through their meals. Some eagerly dug in, the greasy slop of prison food familiar and comforting, while others merely poked at their portions, distracted by the relentless monotony of their existence. None of them knew the danger that lay within the meal. It was only food, after all—something they'd eaten countless times before without issue. But for the few who consumed the tainted portions entirely, the outcome would be far from ordinary.

Hours passed, and it began slowly. A ripple of discomfort spread among those who had finished their meals. It started with a dull nausea, a strange heaviness in the stomach that couldn't be shaken off. At first, some inmates dismissed it as indigestion, a reaction to the low-quality food they were forced to eat. But then, the symptoms worsened.

One man, a large inmate with a history of violent behavior, suddenly gripped his chest. His face turned ashen, sweat beading on his brow as he staggered to his feet. He was quickly overcome with dizziness, his breathing shallow and ragged, and he collapsed against the wall of his cell. His body twitched, seizing in an uncontrollable spasm. Other inmates, who had witnessed his fall, shouted in panic, banging on their bars for attention.

Within minutes, more inmates began to suffer the same symptoms. Their throats constricted, making it impossible to draw a proper breath. Some coughed violently, gasping for air, while others collapsed into unconsciousness. Panic spread like wildfire through the facility. Guards rushed to the cells, yelling orders, but they were powerless to stop the chaos. Medical staff, equally unprepared for the situation, scrambled to tend to the ailing prisoners. They had no idea what was happening—no idea what had caused the sudden, violent onset of symptoms. The prison was quickly overwhelmed, chaos rising as more and more inmates began to show signs of distress.

As medical personnel worked desperately to stabilize the victims, the situation only worsened. The few prisoners who managed to remain conscious were slipping into shock, their bodies fighting to survive against a poison they didn't even know they had ingested. It didn't take long before the first few men died, the cause of death a mystery to those trying to save them. Their bodies were lifeless, their faces frozen in terror, their last moments spent gasping for a breath they would never take.

Katya sat in the dim light of her apartment, her laptop casting a cold glow on her face as she watched it all unfold in real time. The details were unfolding before her eyes, and the quiet thrill of it washed over her like a wave. She leaned back in her chair, a sense of satisfaction in her chest. This was it. This was the beginning of the new order. The first step in her meticulously planned experiment had been executed perfectly. She had taken control of life and death with the precision of a surgeon, and now the world would begin to feel the impact.

The clock on the wall ticked steadily, reminding her that it wouldn't be long before the investigation started. The first whispers of confusion would soon turn into a full-blown inquiry. The medical teams would be baffled, unable to pinpoint the cause. By the time they discovered what had really happened, it would be too late. She had covered every angle, prepared for every possible outcome. There was no way they could trace it back to her, no way they could connect the dots before it was too late. She would be long gone by then—another name on a list, another ghost in the machine.

But even as Katya reveled in her success, there was something that niggled at the back of her mind. **Étienne Lemoine.**

She hadn't heard the last of him. The investigative journalist was getting closer, piecing together the puzzle she had worked so carefully to assemble. His eyes were sharp, his instincts razor-edged, and though she had anticipated many variables in her grand scheme, Étienne was an unpredictable factor. His pursuit of truth was relentless, and it seemed as if he was beginning to sense that something much bigger was at play. Something darker.

But Katya was unshaken. She had already foreseen his every move, already predicted his methods. She knew his type—driven, stubborn, a man of logic and reason. She had studied him, understood how he thought, and had already planted the perfect distractions to lead him astray. It was only a matter of time before he fell into her trap. She would let him get close, let him think he was uncovering something important, let him believe he was winning.

Then, when he was within reach of the truth, she would strike.

The smile that flickered at the corners of her lips was sharp, deliberate. It wasn't just about the killings, nor was it merely about control. This was something far more intimate, something personal. Étienne had no clue what he was really facing. He would be her ultimate trial. And when the moment arrived, she would make sure his story ended just like the rest. With nothing.

A First Encounter—The Interview

Étienne Lemoine's office was dimly lit, the walls cluttered with papers, photographs, and newspaper clippings —all the detritus of a man who had spent years chasing stories that others would shy away from. The only light in the room came from the dull glow of his desk lamp, casting long shadows across the floor. He leaned forward, eyes fixed on the documents Claire had handed him. He'd known the risk of working with her, but Claire was one of the few people he trusted in the world of investigative journalism. She had always been reliable, even when her sources had been shaky.

But now, as he scanned the papers, his pulse quickened. What she had uncovered sent a chill crawling up his spine. The death toll in the prison system was climbing, but it wasn't random. No, this had been calculated. The pattern was unmistakable, and Claire had put it together.

"Several inmates," she said, her voice low, almost wary, "died after eating meals from the same supplier. The cause of death wasn't immediately clear. Respiratory failure. Cardiac arrest. Nothing anyone expected."

Étienne glanced up at her, his brow furrowing. "And the complaints?"

"Anonymous. They came from inside the prisons. People who noticed something wasn't right with the food. But the complaints got buried, dismissed as paranoia or coincidence. Until now." Claire shifted nervously in her seat, her eyes darting to the door. "Someone's been keeping it quiet. Whoever's behind this... they're covering their tracks, Étienne."

He leaned back in his chair, his fingers drumming steadily against the wood. "That's what worries me," he murmured, more to himself than to her. A growing unease settled over him, like a shadow lingering just out of sight.

Claire handed him more papers, her hands trembling slightly as she did. They were pages of food delivery schedules, dates, and invoices, all filled with seemingly innocent details about the distribution process. But Étienne's sharp eyes were already scanning for the cracks. He didn't need to be told; his gut told him this wasn't just a simple case of poor management or negligence. There was something deliberate here. Something that didn't add up.

Then he saw it—repeatedly. The name that kept appearing on the documents. **Katya Vasilieva.**

It stood out like a red flag. The name appeared linked to the food distributor's registration, but there was no clear explanation of who she was, or why she was involved. The information on her was sparse, almost nonexistent, but Étienne's experience told him that was often the case with people who operated in the shadows.

There was something disturbingly clean about her name. Too clean. A blank slate where there should have been more evidence, more history, more connections. His instincts screamed at him—this was no coincidence. She was central to everything.

Étienne's fingers hovered over the papers for a moment, his gaze fixed on the name. Something about it gnawed at him. He wasn't sure why, but he couldn't shake the feeling that she was more than just a name on a list. Katya Vasilieva was the key to the whole thing—he could feel it in his bones. But how? And why?

Before he could ask anything further, Claire spoke again, her voice tinged with uncertainty. "Étienne, be careful. Whoever's behind this... they're not just tampering with the food. They're erasing their tracks in ways you can't even fathom. I don't know if you're prepared for how far this goes."

Étienne met her eyes, his expression firm. "I'm ready," he replied softly. His voice was steady, though there was a flicker of something dangerous in his chest. "If they think I'll stop now, they're wrong."

Claire gave him a knowing look. She had seen this before—the stubborn determination in Étienne's eyes when he was on the scent of something bigger than he had anticipated. "Just promise me you'll be careful," she said.

Étienne nodded. "I always am."

The Hunt Begins

As Étienne walked away from the meeting, the weight of the investigation pressed on him like a heavy cloak. The clues were stacking up, the pieces beginning to click together, but every instinct in him warned that he was only scratching the surface. He needed more information—he needed to go deeper.

Back in his cramped Paris apartment, Étienne sat at his desk, his fingers tracing over the documents once more. The name **Katya Vasilieva** refused to leave his mind. She was the connection he needed to unravel the entire mystery, but the more he researched, the more elusive she became. There was nothing about her that was straightforward. No public records. No trail. Nothing to indicate how she was tied to the food supplier, or to the deaths that had followed.

But Étienne wasn't one to back down. He had spent years tracking down leads that others had abandoned, and if he was going to get to the truth, he would have to find out who she was, and why she was involved. Every lead pointed to her, but still, something about the case didn't sit right. It was too perfect. Too orchestrated. Someone was playing a game—he just didn't know the rules yet.

As he closed his laptop, Étienne's mind raced with possibilities. He was closing in on something big, and he could feel the rush of anticipation in his blood. But something else tugged at him—a quiet sense of dread. Whoever was behind this, they weren't just killers. They were calculating, intelligent, and ruthless. And they had already started to notice him.

In the dim silence of his apartment, Étienne's hand

hovered over the phone. The investigation had already put him on the radar, and he knew there was no turning back now. Katya Vasilieva was the key to everything, and the hunt was just beginning. But with every answer, the risk of what he might uncover grew. Whoever was behind this would stop at nothing to protect their secrets.

And Katya... Katya wasn't just an ordinary player. She was the architect of all of this.

Across the world, miles away, Katya's own heart was pounding, her mind buzzing with thoughts of Étienne. She had been careful, meticulous in covering her tracks. But now, he was onto her—digging deeper into the story.

It was a challenge. A game. And Katya always won her games.

Her fingers hovered over her own laptop. The pieces were in place. She had control. Étienne might be clever, but he was no match for her. She would lead him on, let him chase false leads, and then, just as she always did, she would make him disappear.

She wasn't worried. She had already planned her next move. Étienne would chase her, but he would never catch her.

5

THE INVESTIGATION BEGINS

Paris, France - Late 2010s

Étienne Lemoine sat hunched at his desk in his small Paris apartment, the clutter around him a testament to the intensity of his obsession. Papers were strewn across the floor, notebooks filled with scribbled thoughts, diagrams, and theories lay open, each page looking like the workings of a mind desperate to solve a puzzle. Multiple laptops hummed in the background, screens flickering with the details of his investigation into the mysterious deaths sweeping through U.S. prisons. The air was thick with the weight of his frustration. The answers were always just beyond his reach, and the more he uncovered, the more questions arose.

The deaths were mounting. There was no denying that anymore. The newspapers back in the U.S. were filled with headlines about the rising body count in correctional facilities—an alarming number of inmates dropping dead under suspicious circumstances. And the medical staff, usually quick to label the cause as natural or drug-related, were stumped. No known diseases could explain the rapid, violent nature of the deaths. Toxicology reports were as elusive as ever—nothing conclusive, nothing solid to explain what was happening. The forensic pathologists couldn't even agree on the symptoms. Some prisoners died with signs of suffocation, others with internal hemorrhaging, while some showed no physical signs at all, dying seemingly in their sleep.

Étienne stared at his screen, furrowing his brow. He'd been piecing this together for weeks, and yet, the puzzle refused to make sense. The timeline didn't line up with any known poisoning methods, nor did the victims' profiles match any typical pattern of prison violence. His fingers tapped restlessly against the desk. *What was it?*

He rubbed his face, his patience fraying. His mind, though, kept going back to one thing—the food. Prison meals were the common denominator, but beyond that, he couldn't quite make the connection. What was the link between the food and the bizarre, slow-developing deaths?

Suddenly, a single phrase flashed in his mind: *food supplier.* He had noted it weeks ago, but hadn't yet dug deeper. He opened his folder, scattered with leads and scraps of information, and began typing furiously on his laptop, the sound of keys clicking in rapid succession. He brought up a list of food distribution companies contracted to U.S. correctional facilities, and his eyes scanned the names, but there was one that stood out like a neon sign.

Katya Vasilieva.

The name struck him like a hammer. He'd come across it before, hidden in the corners of some of the documents he had been reviewing—nothing overt, just a passing mention, a name on a vendor's list, an inconspicuous reference in a background check on the food suppliers. At first, he hadn't given it much attention. There were thousands of names on similar lists. But now, looking at it again, *this* name seemed different. It felt *too clean*, too precise in its placement, as if it had been intentionally tucked away, as if it were always meant to be found but only at the right time.

Étienne felt a cold chill creep down his spine as he began opening every document he had on her. A search through various government databases revealed startling gaps in her history. Katya Vasilieva had lived in the U.S. for nearly four years, but there was nothing before that. No family history. No records of where she came from or why she was in the States. Her immigration papers were spotless—unremarkable. It was as if she had appeared out of nowhere, a blank slate, with no apparent reason for her existence in the U.S. beyond the food distribution business. No relatives. No personal life.

And yet, the more he looked, the more undeniable it became. Her name kept showing up in connection with government contracts, food distribution companies, and even medical supply chains. She was involved in several layers of the prison system's logistics, from meal delivery to medicine, but she was never directly in the spotlight. The records on her were pristine—no red flags, no warnings, no investigations. Just clean, bureaucratic paper trails that seemed to lead nowhere. Except, now that he was looking, it was clear that they led to *her*.

Katya Vasilieva was everywhere. And yet, no one seemed to know anything about her.

Étienne's pulse quickened. The more he dug, the more he began to feel like he was staring at the final piece of a jigsaw puzzle that had eluded him for weeks. He had been so focused on the symptoms, on the deaths, and the pattern of poisoned meals, that he hadn't once questioned the source—the person orchestrating this.

Her name was there, in the background, in the margins. But now, it *was* the story.

Étienne quickly jotted down some more notes, his mind racing with possibilities. She wasn't just another name in a sea of logistics and corporate contracts. There was something deeply off about her. *What was her endgame? Why was she involved in something as dangerous as this?* The deaths in the prisons—they weren't random. This wasn't the work of some disorganized killer or a syndicate looking to profit off of chaos. No, this was a *carefully* orchestrated plan. And someone had put it in motion.

His instincts screamed at him, louder than before. She was the architect. Katya Vasilieva had designed this entire operation. Her hands were all over it—hidden, masked by the clean-cut image she presented, but she was there, pulling the strings.

But the bigger question remained: *Why?*

Étienne sat back in his chair, his thoughts a swirl of confusion and clarity. He needed to find out everything about her. How she worked, who she knew, what her motives were. It was time to get close. He had to follow her trail back to its source, but every step felt like it was taking him deeper into a rabbit hole that could end in one of two ways: the truth or his own undoing.

He knew the risks. He had faced danger before, but this... this was different. This was a well-constructed, dangerous game—and Katya Vasilieva was the one who held all the pieces.

Étienne leaned forward again, fingers poised over the keyboard. There was no going back now. He was on the hunt, and he wouldn't stop until he had the answers—no matter where they led him.

. . .

The Poisoning Crisis Spreads

Back in the U.S., a tense cloud of uncertainty hung over the prison system. What had begun as a handful of mysterious deaths had spiraled into a full-blown crisis. The corrections departments were under intense scrutiny, as more and more inmates began dying under suspicious circumstances. Investigations had been launched, but they were futile. The cause of the deaths was elusive, slipping through the cracks of their analysis. No one could pinpoint what was truly happening—there were no traces of the usual poisons or toxins, no obvious signs of foul play. It was as if something invisible had entered the system, spreading its grip silently, mercilessly. The inmates didn't show symptoms of poisoning—they simply dropped dead. It was quick, efficient, and utterly baffling.

Hospitals were overwhelmed, medical staff scrambling to identify what was happening. The victims didn't exhibit the usual symptoms of poisoning: no visible signs of internal bleeding, no obvious traces of toxins in their systems. At first, authorities suspected some form of foodborne illness or an outbreak of something akin to botulism, but even these possibilities were ruled out. Some theorized a more sinister cause—a bioterrorism attack, a rogue agent of some kind who had infiltrated the system to enact mass death. Others suggested it could be the work of a highly organized and elusive serial killer within the prison, picking off inmates one by one with clinical precision. Every day, new reports flooded in, but each left authorities no closer to the truth.

Media outlets, hungry for any sort of explanation, ran wild with a litany of theories, none of them grounded in fact. Conspiracy after conspiracy spread like wildfire, from claims that the deaths were the result of a coordinated attack by a radical group to whispers of a vengeful ex-convict in the midst of a personal vendetta. The public was in a state of panic, and the pressure on law enforcement only grew heavier.

Katya, sitting in her minimalist apartment, watched it all unfold on the screen of her laptop. Her face remained calm, but her eyes gleamed with satisfaction, a cold, calculated satisfaction. The chaos, the confusion—it was all part of her plan. She knew what was happening, she had orchestrated it, and to her, this was just the beginning. Each death was like a note in a symphony, each life snuffed out a small, calculated sacrifice on her path to something far greater.

She leaned back in her chair, the faint hum of the laptop's fan the only sound in the quiet room. A small, almost imperceptible smile curved her lips as she watched the authorities scramble. The deaths, treated as isolated outbreaks, were only the start. There would be more. There would always be more. Each victim was a step forward, a step closer to her ultimate goal. She could feel it now— power thrumming through her veins, a raw, electrifying energy that coursed through her as she watched the world struggle to find its footing.

In her mind, the lives she claimed weren't just deaths— they were *offerings*. Every person she took was another piece in her grand design, another soul claimed to fuel her rise. This wasn't just about vengeance. It was about control. Power. She was remaking the world in her image, one carefully timed death at a time.

But despite her satisfaction, Katya knew that the game wasn't over. There was one loose end still dangling on the edge of her plans—Étienne Lemoine.

She had been tracking him, of course. She knew the French investigative journalist was getting closer, piecing together the puzzle with alarming speed. He had started connecting the dots, picking up on the subtle trail she had left behind. His instincts were sharp, his curiosity unrelenting. He had quickly zeroed in on the fact that the deaths were somehow linked to the food distribution system, and from there, he had begun to make dangerous connections.

It wasn't that she had underestimated him—it was simply that she hadn't expected him to move so quickly. His persistence was admirable, but ultimately futile. He would follow the wrong leads, she was sure of it. He had already begun to dig into the food supply chain, and she had prepared for that. His search would lead him in circles, always just out of reach of the truth.

Still, there was a nagging feeling in the back of her mind. Étienne was smart. Smarter than most. He might have made some early missteps, but that didn't mean he wouldn't catch up to her eventually. He was like a bloodhound, relentless, sniffing at the scent of the truth.

But Katya wasn't worried. Not yet. She had already set her plans in motion, and no matter how close Étienne got, it was already too late. The poison had been spread, the victims were already dying, and the authorities were far too disorganized to connect the dots in time. She had thought of everything—every angle, every move. The investigation would be bungled. False leads would misdirect the police, taking them down rabbit holes and giving her ample time to cover her tracks. By the time anyone had even the faintest idea of what was really going on, she would be long gone. Untouchable.

She turned her attention back to the reports, watching as the death toll continued to rise. The chaos was perfect. It was only a matter of time before Étienne's pursuit of the truth led him into her trap. She would let him get close. Let him think he was winning. And when the time was right, she would destroy him, just like she had destroyed so many others.

The game was still in its early stages, but Katya could already feel the pieces shifting into place. Power was within her reach, and she would stop at nothing to claim it. The world would bow to her—or it would burn.

The First Confrontation

Étienne Lemoine's investigation had brought him to a critical juncture. With the web of deaths spreading across U.S. prisons, his suspicions were growing clearer, but there was still something missing—a concrete lead that would finally pull everything together. His journey had led him across the ocean, under the radar, into a world far removed from his usual Parisian haunts. It wasn't safe, but Étienne had always been good at slipping through the cracks when necessary. His reputation as a relentless investigative journalist had allowed him to build an underground network of contacts, people who knew things and were willing to talk —for the right price or for the right cause.

Through this network, he had secured a meeting with someone who could provide vital insight into the recent deaths: Brian Peterson, a former prison official with years of experience in the system. Peterson was a nervous wreck, his hands shaking as he tried to steady the papers scattered across his office. The once-dominant man in charge of logistics had clearly seen too much in recent weeks—too much that he couldn't unsee. He had quit his job after the string of inmate deaths had spiraled out of control, each one more baffling and horrific than the last.

Peterson's office, tucked away in a grim, dilapidated building that housed the state's prison records, smelled of stale coffee and old paperwork. It was a far cry from the clean, polished offices that Étienne was accustomed to. The fluorescent lights flickered overhead as Peterson shuffled through a pile of notes, clearly rattled, trying to organize his thoughts into something coherent.

"It's all wrong, man. All wrong. These guys—these criminals—they're supposed to be in prison to pay for their sins, but now they're dying like animals," Peterson mumbled, his voice trembling as he glanced over his shoulder. He leaned in closer to Étienne, lowering his voice to a near whisper, as though the walls themselves might betray him. "They were supposed to rot in here, not... not like this."

Étienne watched him closely, sensing the deeper fear behind the words. Peterson wasn't just rattled by the deaths; he was scared. And not the usual kind of fear that prison staff experienced from time to time, but something deeper, more profound. This was the kind of fear you felt when you knew that something was deeply wrong, but you couldn't quite put your finger on it.

Leaning forward, Étienne's tone was calm but firm, his voice barely a whisper. "You said these deaths weren't natural. How many of them were tied to the same food supplier?"

Peterson swallowed hard, his eyes darting to the side as though he were looking for an escape route. He knew he was about to say something dangerous. The kind of revelation that might unravel everything—and leave him exposed.

"Most of them, at least those who were alive long

enough to eat..." Peterson's words trailed off as he glanced nervously out the window. The street outside was quiet, but it was as if he feared the wrong person might be listening. "Whoever did this... they're smart, man. Too smart. The food's not the issue. It's what's in the food." He shuddered involuntarily, as though the thought of it physically repulsed him. "And it's not just one prison. It's everywhere. The same suppliers, the same method... it's like they're systematically poisoning the entire system, one meal at a time."

Étienne's mind raced. A methodical, widespread campaign of poisoning? It sounded almost too calculated to be real. The scale of what Peterson was describing was enormous, far beyond the scope of any single individual. Étienne had assumed the deaths were isolated events, a rogue attacker or a botched plot gone wrong. But this was something entirely different. This was a conspiracy—a deliberate, coordinated effort to wipe out inmates, not with guns or violence, but with poison.

A chill crept up Étienne's spine as Peterson's words settled in. It wasn't just one or two prisons; it was a systemic problem, a campaign that spanned multiple institutions. And someone was orchestrating it from behind the scenes, leaving no trace, covering their tracks with such precision that it was impossible for anyone to see the bigger picture. It was almost like an invisible hand, moving the pieces on a chessboard, one meal at a time.

Étienne's mind flashed back to the earlier reports, the strange deaths he had been tracking, and the inexplicable spikes in fatalities within certain prison facilities. He'd been piecing together small details, but Peterson's testimony confirmed what Étienne had feared all along: these deaths weren't accidents. They weren't the result of some botched gang-related violence or a run-of-the-mill prison riot. They were intentional. And the method of execution was something far more insidious than anything he'd imagined.

"Whoever's behind this," Peterson continued, his voice barely audible now, "they've got everything figured out. They know how to cover their tracks. You can't trace it, you can't even *see* it. It's in the food, but the victims—they just fall dead. And nobody knows why." He looked down at his hands, his eyes haunted. "I've seen the reports—people are starting to talk. But the higher-ups don't want this to get out. They don't want the public to know what's really going on."

Étienne's eyes narrowed as the last piece clicked into place. There was more to this than just a simple food contamination. Someone had orchestrated these deaths to occur in the most controlled and undetectable way possible. This was no ordinary poisoning. Whoever was behind it had designed the toxin to evade all detection, manipulating the system to carry out their plan without anyone noticing until it was far too late.

He looked at Peterson with steely determination, pushing aside the unease that threatened to overwhelm him. "How did you get involved in this? What made you leave your position?"

Peterson shifted uncomfortably in his seat, his fingers fumbling with the papers on his desk. "I—I couldn't stand it anymore. It was like watching something evil take hold, and I just couldn't keep pretending that I didn't know what was happening. I started digging around, looking at the food suppliers, asking questions. And that's when I found the link. The deaths? They're all connected to one supplier —*the* supplier that handles food for *every* major prison in the system. It's not just random people dying. These are calculated hits."

Étienne's pulse quickened as Peterson's words sank in. He could feel the gravity of the situation pressing down on him. This wasn't just another investigative piece to unravel; this was a ticking time bomb. And someone, somewhere, was playing a very dangerous game.

He stood up abruptly, gathering the papers Peterson had handed him. He had to move quickly. This wasn't just a story anymore. It was a race against time to stop something far worse from unfolding.

As he left Peterson's office, Étienne's thoughts were already racing ahead, piecing together the puzzle with a new urgency. Whoever was behind this wasn't just targeting criminals—they were targeting the very heart of the system. And he was about to become the one person who could stop it all.

But what Étienne didn't know, as he walked into the cold night air, was that he had just made himself a target. The person responsible was watching him, and she was already planning her next move.

Katya's Next Move

Back in her New York apartment, Katya was a whirlwind of calculated energy, her mind consumed by the next phase of her grand experiment. The initial success of her poisonings had already set the wheels of chaos in motion, but she wasn't content with just watching the bodies pile up. For Katya, this was never about simple revenge or killing for the sake of killing—this was about power. About control. About reshaping the world in her vision. And she knew that to achieve the god-like status she craved, she needed to master not just death, but perception.

The growing crisis in the U.S. prison system was feeding her carefully constructed narrative, but it was beginning to draw unwanted attention. The media was starting to ask questions, and though they were still grasping at straws, it wouldn't be long before someone connected the dots. Someone like Étienne Lemoine. His relentless investigation was a threat to everything she had worked for. She had anticipated his probing mind and knew that his persistence would eventually bring him dangerously close to the truth. And she couldn't afford for that to happen. Not yet.

Katya understood that, in a world of information overload, controlling the media narrative was just as powerful as controlling life and death itself. It was time to manipulate the media—turn their questions into distractions, their speculations into false trails. She would become the shadowy force behind the storm, never revealing her true identity, but always orchestrating the chaos. The media wasn't just an external force in her plan; it was a tool she could bend to her will.

She began with subtlety, using her vast hacking expertise to infiltrate major news outlets. Journalists were so desperate for information about the mysterious deaths that they would follow any lead, no matter how dubious. Katya planted false reports, emails, and interviews from fabricated sources that twisted the narrative in the direction she wanted. The deaths weren't part of a carefully executed plan, she implied—they were simply the result of an unfortunate outbreak. Mismanagement, negligence, maybe even a product of prison conditions. She steered them away from the truth: that there was a mastermind at work behind the scenes, pulling the strings.

But that wasn't enough for her. She needed to go further. She needed to give the public a voice—a voice that would echo her philosophy of death, justice, and retribution. It would be subtle but powerful. Katya created an anonymous blog, "The Death Whisperer," an online platform where she could freely share her twisted insights, opinions, and philosophy on the unfolding prison crisis.

The blog became a shadowy corner of the internet, where lurkers from all walks of life stumbled upon it, their curiosity piqued by its cryptic, philosophical musings. At first, the posts were innocuous—disguised as abstract commentary on life, death, and society. But as the deaths grew, so did her influence. Katya began weaving stories and theories about the nature of punishment, power, and how the criminal justice system had failed to serve true justice. She talked about cleansing the world of its undesirables, about the purity of death, and how the balance of power needed to be reset. Her writing was poetic, her words dripping with a sense of righteous fury. It was the perfect camouflage—an alluring, intellectual smokescreen for the darkness she had created. She was no longer just an anonymous assassin. Now, she was a philosopher, a messenger of death, speaking to the world through her cryptic posts.

The blog's following grew rapidly. People were drawn to her words—those who felt disconnected, disillusioned with society's failures. They saw her as a voice of reason, someone who understood the true cost of justice and the price of power.

Katya smiled darkly as she read the comments on her posts, her fingers gliding over the keyboard. She reveled in her growing influence. But even as she basked in her success, something gnawed at the back of her mind. Étienne.

She had known he would catch wind of her work, eventually. After all, Étienne Lemoine was no ordinary journalist

—he was relentless, sharp, and driven by an almost obsessive need to uncover the truth. Her every move had been designed to keep him off balance, to keep him guessing. But now, as the media storm escalated, his presence was becoming more of a threat.

Her mind churned with strategies. Étienne wasn't just following the story; he was close. He was on her trail, and that meant it was time to shift gears. Katya had already laid false leads for him to follow—clues that would send him chasing down rabbit holes, distracting him from the real trail she had left hidden. She'd planted subtle misinformation on his encrypted emails, fake data files that would lead him to wrong conclusions. She'd even manipulated the timelines of certain prison meals to confuse the chain of evidence, making it seem like the deaths were the result of random, isolated events.

But all that might not be enough. Étienne's instincts were sharp, and his tenacity meant he wouldn't stop until he was standing face-to-face with the truth.

So Katya took her next step. She knew Étienne's network of contacts well—she had already studied his every move, every lead, every ally. And among those allies was someone she could use. A former associate of Étienne's, someone he trusted, someone who had been feeding him key information for months. Katya had been keeping an eye on this person, waiting for the right moment to strike. And now, with Étienne getting dangerously close to unmasking her, she reached out.

She sent a carefully crafted message to this contact, posing as an insider who had stumbled upon vital information. The message was deliberately vague, enough to entice curiosity, but with just enough detail to make it seem credible. It was a perfect setup—an opportunity for this contact to unknowingly feed Étienne the wrong information, leading him further down the wrong path. The contact would never suspect it was Katya pulling the strings.

She knew this would buy her time. Time to strengthen her position, time to escalate the next stage of her plan. By the time Étienne began to realize the false trails he had been chasing, it would be too late. She would be long gone —just a shadow in the world's chaos, watching from the sidelines as the crisis spiraled out of control.

But what Katya didn't realize was that the game had only just begun. Étienne was already one step ahead. And soon, she would learn that even her careful manipulations might not be enough to keep him in the dark forever.

The Investigative Journalist's Dilemma

Étienne sat in his cramped hotel room, the dim light of his laptop screen flickering in the darkness. The exhaustion was starting to show—his eyes bloodshot, his face haggard, his fingers stiff from typing for hours on end. He had been chasing this story for weeks, piecing together fragments of information, following leads that always seemed to end in dead ends. The mystery had become a maze, and Étienne was beginning to lose his bearings. The more he uncovered, the less he understood. The more he followed the twisted paths that had been laid out before him, the further he seemed to stray from the truth.

The weight of the investigation was starting to wear on him, and he could feel it—a growing sense that he was losing his grip. He had always taken pride in his ability to see through the deception, to cut through the smoke and mirrors and find the truth. But now, as the pieces of the case failed to align, he was starting to question whether he was pursuing mere shadows, or something far darker, far more lethal. Something that didn't want to be discovered.

It wasn't just the overwhelming sense of confusion. It was the feeling that someone was always watching, always one step ahead. Misdirection had become a constant companion in his investigation. Every time he thought he was close to an answer, a new layer of deception was peeled back, and he found himself deeper in the labyrinth, with fewer and fewer clues to guide him.

He thought back to the tip-off he had received earlier that day. It had seemed like a breakthrough. The source had been reliable—someone within the prison system with information about a corrupt official who had ties to the food supplier that seemed to be at the heart of the deaths. Étienne had traced the lead to a rundown address on the outskirts of the city, and he had hoped that this time, he might find something concrete. But when he arrived, there was nothing. No official, no documents, no answers. Just an empty building, and a gnawing sense of betrayal.

It wasn't the first time this had happened. The closer he got, the more elusive the truth became. The false leads, the dead ends, the people who refused to talk, who had been silenced, or worse, manipulated into saying nothing. Étienne couldn't shake the feeling that he was being toyed with. That someone, or something, was playing a game with him.

As he stared at the screen in front of him, a sinking feeling settled in his stomach. He had long suspected that this case wasn't just about an outbreak of random deaths— it had always felt more orchestrated, more deliberate. The scale of it was unlike anything he'd ever encountered. This wasn't just a case of a rogue food supplier or a few corrupt officials. This was a carefully constructed narrative. And as

Étienne pieced together the fragmented puzzle in front of him, one name kept coming back to the forefront: Katya Vasilieva.

She was the missing piece. The one link he couldn't fully understand but couldn't ignore. The more he researched her, the more his gut told him she was the key to everything. But why? Why would someone like her—someone with no known ties to the criminal world, with no obvious reason for being involved in such a dark conspiracy—be at the heart of this? The questions only multiplied the more he uncovered, and the answers seemed to slip further from his grasp.

It was then that Étienne's phone rang, pulling him from his spiraling thoughts. The caller ID flashed Claire's name. His heart skipped a beat. Claire had been his contact within the prison system, a source who had provided valuable information, but she had been growing more and more anxious as the investigation had deepened. Her warnings had been growing more urgent. Étienne hesitated for a moment before picking up, sensing that this call was going to be different.

"Étienne," Claire's voice crackled over the line, thin with panic. She sounded frantic, her words tumbling out in a rush. "You're getting too close. You don't understand who you're dealing with. This... this isn't just about the deaths. This isn't just about some twisted food supplier or a few corrupt officials. Katya... she's not just a killer. She's building something. A system. A world, Étienne. And you're in it now. Get out. Now."

Her voice shook with fear, the words tumbling out in a broken whisper as though she could feel the weight of her warning, knowing that it might be the last piece of truth she could offer him.

Étienne's mind raced, but he couldn't make sense of it. *Building something? A world? What did that even mean?* His mind had always operated in concrete terms—facts, evidence, logical conclusions. But Claire's words weren't logical. They didn't fit with anything he had uncovered. And yet, a sense of dread curled in his chest. What was it that Claire knew, that she was too afraid to say?

"Claire," Étienne said, his voice steady but urgent. "What do you mean? What is she building?"

But before Claire could answer, the line went dead. The sudden silence on the other end of the phone was deafening, and Étienne was left staring at the screen in disbelief. He redialed her number, but it went straight to voicemail. His stomach churned. *What the hell is happening?*

He sat back in his chair, his mind spinning. The words Claire had said echoed in his mind: *You're in it now.* She hadn't just been warning him about the danger of getting too close to Katya. She had been warning him about something far deeper, something more insidious. And as the gravity of her warning settled in, Étienne realized that he had made a fatal mistake.

He wasn't just investigating a story anymore. He was part of it. He had been pulled into Katya's world, a world she had been carefully crafting for years. And no matter how hard he tried, no matter how many false leads he chased, he wasn't going to be able to escape it.

The truth had always been elusive. But now, it was clearer than ever. Katya wasn't just pulling the strings behind the deaths in the prison system. She was constructing a new reality, one where she would hold all the power, and the rest of the world would play her game. And Étienne was already trapped in it, whether he realized it or not.

As the weight of this realization pressed down on him, Étienne's phone buzzed again. This time, the message was simple, and it sent a cold shiver down his spine: *You're too late, Étienne. There is no going back.*

He froze. For the first time in his career, he wasn't sure how to proceed. Would he be able to stop her? Or had he already lost?

6

KATYA'S DELUSIONS

New York City, Early 2020s

The apartment was silent, save for the soft hum of the city outside—distant, muffled, as if the entire world had been momentarily held in suspension. The air inside felt dense, charged with the weight of purpose. Every corner of the room was bathed in the pale glow of the desk lamp, and the only movement came from Katya's fingers, drumming an impatient rhythm against the polished wood of the desk. She was focused, her gaze unwavering as it locked onto the screen in front of her.

Her latest creation was now live. The blog post had been uploaded with the precision of a masterstroke, her words cutting through the noise of the digital world like a blade. Each sentence, every word, had been carefully constructed to leave an impact. *Cryptic, provocative,* yet *undeniably powerful.* Katya knew the effect it would have. She could almost hear the ripple of intrigue, the shiver of recognition from those who would read it. She wasn't just writing. She was planting a seed—a seed that would grow, burrow into the minds of her audience, and slowly, inevitably, take root.

She leaned back in her chair, closing her eyes for a moment, and allowed herself to feel the satisfaction of her work. She had sent a message. The words would echo across the ether, traveling through the digital veins of the world, spreading her vision. She was a force now—a force of life and death, and the world would soon know her name.

The title of the post, *The Path to Immortality*, lingered in her mind as if it were a mantra, a truth she had uncovered and was now ready to share with those who would listen. The post itself was like a dark sermon, a manifesto of power cloaked in philosophical and historical musings. She spoke of history, of men and women who had shaped the world through violence, domination, and the manipulation of life and death. Figures like Hitler and Stalin, men who had ascended beyond the realm of ordinary mortals. Men who had gained godlike status not through wisdom, not through kindness or virtue, but through *blood*. The blood of millions.

In Katya's mind, they were gods. Gods, not because of any supernatural power, but because they had controlled the most primal force in existence: life and death. And through the blood they shed, they had transcended the human condition. They had shaped the world with their cruelty, and in doing so, they had achieved something no other mortal could fathom—*immortality*.

The deaths they caused had been the keys to their power. The souls of the dead had bowed before them, their existence erased from the world, but their spirits forever bound to the ones who had taken them. And now, Katya was walking that same path. She wasn't just a murderer.

She was a creator, a goddess-in-waiting, carving her way through the veil of mortality and into something far greater, something beyond human understanding. She wasn't just making history; she was becoming history.

Her fingers hovered over the keyboard again, the cursor blinking on the blank space at the bottom of the screen. A fleeting thought passed through her mind: Should she add more? Should she elaborate on the driving force behind her actions? Her carefully executed plan—one that had unfolded for months—wasn't just about power. It wasn't even just about the deaths themselves. It was about resurrection.

She had never fully shared her true motivations before, not even to her most loyal followers. But now, perhaps it was time. Should she explain how her actions were, in a sense, her way of resurrecting her brother Donovan? The one person she had truly loved. The one person who had always understood her. The one person who had been taken from her, and in his death, had given her the strength to move forward.

His death had been the catalyst, the spark that ignited everything. She could hear his voice in her mind, soft and encouraging, whispering in the spaces between her thoughts. *You're doing the right thing, Katya. You're creating a new world. A better world.*

Maybe she could add that. She could explain how Donovan's soul had guided her to this place, how his memory had been the fuel that had driven her to such heights. His death had given her purpose. But as her fingers hovered over the keys, she hesitated. No. It wasn't necessary. It wasn't time yet. The world didn't need to understand everything. Not yet. She had already given them a glimpse of her vision.

The seeds had been planted. Her words, now out in the world, would begin to grow. They would spread, seeping into the subconscious minds of those who read them, making them question their own beliefs, their own understanding of life and death. They would begin to wonder about the nature of power, about the meaning of sacrifice, about the delicate balance between creation and destruction. Some would follow her vision willingly, others would resist, but in the end, it didn't matter.

Katya wasn't interested in the trivial concerns of those who couldn't see her genius. She was moving beyond them, creating something far greater than anyone could comprehend. The world would either follow her vision or be swept aside by the unstoppable force of her will.

With a final, satisfied glance at her blog post, Katya clicked the "publish" button. The message had been sent. The world would respond in time. And she, standing in the shadows, would be waiting.

Étienne's Realization

Étienne sat hunched over his desk, the flickering light of his computer screen casting harsh shadows across his face. His eyes were bloodshot from sleepless nights, his mind clouded by the constant, relentless flood of information. Weeks of investigation had drained him physically and emotionally. Each day felt like a weight on his chest, his sense of purpose the only thing keeping him tethered to his work.

But he couldn't stop. Not now. Every time he thought he was close to uncovering the truth, something pulled him back—something deeper, darker, and more sinister than he had ever anticipated. The pieces he had been gathering didn't fit neatly into any logical pattern. They twisted and warped, evading his understanding, until it all seemed to collapse into something worse than a conspiracy—it was an orchestrated, intentional descent into madness.

His eyes glazed over the documents in front of him—a fresh set of corruption files that had surfaced from his latest source. The data was damning. The connections were undeniable. They tied directly to Katya's food distribution network. This was the breakthrough he'd been waiting for, the moment when everything would finally come into focus. But instead of feeling the exhilaration of nearing the truth, all Étienne felt was a deep, gnawing unease.

He ran a hand through his hair and leaned back in his chair, his muscles stiff from hours of sitting. The more he uncovered, the more he realized that the closer he got to Katya, the tighter the walls around him seemed to close in. It was like a trap. Every file he opened, every lead he followed, felt like it was designed to push him further into her web, to draw him deeper into a world he was only beginning to understand.

Katya was playing him.

The realization hit him like a cold slap to the face. All along, he had thought he was chasing a killer, a twisted mastermind orchestrating a spree of murders. But now, as the pieces came together, he understood the truth: Katya wasn't just a criminal. She was a puppeteer, pulling the strings of this investigation, manipulating every aspect of it. The media stories that led him down false trails, the fabricated clues in the food supplier's files, even the corruption he'd uncovered—all of it had been meticulously engineered by her. She had known he would come, had known how to lead him in exactly the wrong direction, all the while pushing him closer to her, making him think he was the one in control.

But why? What was her endgame? What was she after? He hadn't figured that out yet, but he felt the weight of it pressing on him, like a shadow looming over everything he did. The more he uncovered, the more it became clear: this was no ordinary case. Katya Vasilieva was not just a killer. She wasn't just a criminal mastermind. She was something far more dangerous—someone with an agenda that was both grandiose and terrifying. Her reach extended far beyond the lives she'd taken. There was something bigger at play here, something that Étienne couldn't yet comprehend.

As if on cue, his phone buzzed. The message flashed on the screen, a single line from Claire.

"Étienne, I've found something that might help. But you need to be careful. She's not who you think she is. Katya—she believes she's going to become something more. She has a vision, a delusional one. You're dealing with someone who's not entirely human in the way she thinks. Get out before it's too late."

Étienne stared at the screen, the words hitting him like a blow to the gut. He had known something was off—he had suspected for a while that there was more to Katya than met the eye. But this... this was something entirely different.

He reread Claire's message, his heart sinking deeper into his chest. Katya didn't just see herself as a murderer. She wasn't merely killing for power, for money, or even for revenge. No. She believed she was destined for something more—something beyond the human realm. A *vision*. Claire's words lingered in his mind, "not entirely human in the way she thinks." What did that mean? Had she lost her grip on reality? Or was she just so consumed by her own delusions of grandeur that she saw herself as some kind of deity?

Étienne felt the edges of his reality begin to blur. He had been following the breadcrumbs, piecing together a puzzle that was quickly becoming a nightmare. The more he thought about it, the clearer it became: this wasn't just about death. This wasn't just about taking lives. This was about something far more sinister. This was about *control*, about bending the world to her will, about transcending the very concept of humanity.

Katya wasn't just a killer—she was on a mission to become something *greater*, something beyond the realm of mere mortals. She wanted to reshape the world in her image, and in her mind, every death, every soul claimed, was a step closer to that transformation. She was forging a path toward immortality, but not in any conventional sense. It was a twisted path, built on suffering and death, but in her mind, it was the only way forward.

Étienne clenched his fists, the weight of Claire's words settling on him like a cold stone. He couldn't back out now. He couldn't stop. He had come too far, and the stakes were higher than ever.

Katya had to be stopped. Before she could claim any more lives. Before she could convince anyone else that her vision was the truth. She had to be brought down before her delusions consumed the world.

Étienne stared at the screen, his mind racing with a newfound urgency. His next move had to be the right one. He couldn't afford to make any more mistakes. The clock was ticking, and Katya was always one step ahead. But he wasn't going to stop. Not now. He would find her. He would stop her. Before it was too late.

. . .

Katya's Growing Power

Katya felt invincible now. A sense of unshakable control pulsed through her veins, stronger than any drug. She had orchestrated the death of dozens, manipulated systems on a global scale, and woven a network of power so subtle, so intricate, that it seemed almost divine. Her influence had spread like an insidious virus, infecting the U.S. prison system, media outlets, and anyone unfortunate enough to become entangled in her web. And yet, it was never enough—she craved more, always more. Power was no longer a distant dream; it was a reality that now lay within her grasp.

Standing in front of her full-length mirror, Katya surveyed her reflection. The woman looking back at her was different now. Her eyes held an intensity that wasn't there before, an unyielding fire. Her skin seemed to glow with an inner light, a presence that radiated from her every pore. She had always been calculated, always been methodical, but now there was something else—something beyond human. Something divine.

She wasn't just Katya Vasilieva anymore. That name—once just a marker of her past, of who she had been—had become a shadow of what she truly was now. She had transcended her former self, shedding it like a snake discarding its skin. She was no longer bound by the limits of human morality or emotion. What was once a cold ambition had now evolved into something far more powerful: a belief in her own divinity.

Her vision of life and death had been warped over time, until she no longer saw herself as a mere killer. No, she was the purifier. Every life she took, every soul she claimed, was part of a sacred ritual. A cleansing process. She had come to believe that the corrupt, the violent, the vile—they had no right to exist. Her hands, stained with blood, were the hands of a goddess. She was carving a path to immortality, to godhood, through death itself. And the souls of the dead weren't just fading away. They were joining her, whispering their secrets into her ears, guiding her actions, giving her strength. With every soul she harvested, her power grew, until it felt as though she were no longer just a woman, but something far older, far more primal—something that had existed since the dawn of time.

The voices that murmured in her mind had become clearer, more distinct. They wanted her to rule. They wanted her to wield power over the living, over the world itself. Every death was a step closer to her ascension. She had already begun planning the next phase—something even grander, something that would shake the very foundation of the world. It would be a plan so catastrophic, so devastating, that it would leave the entire planet at her feet. The death toll would soar. The chaos would be absolute. And in that chaos, she would rise.

Her enemies? They were just obstacles—nothing more than pawns in the grand game she was playing.

But there was one thread left untangled: Étienne Lemoine. He was the only one who had come close to understanding the true scope of her actions. The French journalist had been persistent, digging through the lies and misdirections she had carefully planted for him. He was beginning to connect the dots. That was dangerous. Too dangerous.

She could feel the walls closing in on him, but Étienne was no fool. His instincts were sharp, his methods relentless. She had underestimated him once, but she wouldn't make that mistake again. He was too close to discovering the truth. She had to stop him—permanently.

A cruel smile tugged at Katya's lips as her fingers twitched in anticipation. She had already begun weaving a new plan to deal with Étienne. He thought he was winning, that he was getting closer to her, to the core of her operation. That was exactly how she wanted him to feel. She would play him, manipulate him, like a puppet on a string, leading him deeper into her labyrinth of lies and half-truths. Let him chase her. Let him think he was on the verge of uncovering her. And then—when the time was right—she would strike.

Étienne would never see it coming. He had no idea what he was dealing with. But she knew him. She understood how his mind worked, how he could not resist the lure of the truth. And she would exploit that weakness.

As she thought of him, a new fire lit within her. He would be no different than the rest. Just another victim to be consumed by her growing power. She had already claimed so many lives, but Étienne? He would be the most satisfying of all.

She would let him think he was the hunter, chasing her through the maze of false clues and misdirections. But in reality, she had been the one guiding him all along. Every step he took toward the truth would only lead him further into her grasp. And when she had him cornered, when he was desperate for answers, she would reveal her full power. She would become the force that tore through his world.

And then, Étienne Lemoine would be no more.

In the quiet of her apartment, as her mind raced with plans, Katya felt a surge of excitement flood through her. This was it. This was her moment. The world was on the brink of collapse, and she—she—was the one pulling the strings. She would become a god. And when the world bent the knee before her, she would finally take her rightful place among the immortals.

The game had only just begun, but Katya knew one thing for certain: there was no stopping her now.

The Confrontation

Étienne's breath came in shallow, nervous bursts as he stood in front of the building. Lower Manhattan—old, weathered, and full of secrets. This was where the chase had led him. It had been months of painstaking investigation, countless false leads, and dead ends. But now, standing at the threshold of her world, the final confrontation was at hand. Katya was no longer a shadowy figure—she was the architect of the chaos, the mastermind behind the deaths, the puppeteer who had manipulated the media, the government, and, more than anyone, him.

His gut twisted with a mixture of fear and anticipation. He had tracked her down. He had all the evidence he needed. But as he stepped into the building—a dilapidated, crumbling structure that felt like it had been forgotten by time—he couldn't shake the feeling that he had just walked into something far darker than he had anticipated. It wasn't just a confrontation he was about to face; it was a reckoning with something unnatural.

The hallway was eerily silent as Étienne moved forward. The flickering of a lone overhead bulb cast long, unnerving shadows along the peeling walls. His eyes scanned the space, searching for any signs of life, but there was nothing. It was too quiet, and for a moment, he felt the heavy weight of doubt pressing on him. Was this a trap? Was he walking right into her hands?

The door to Katya's apartment stood slightly open. It wasn't locked, which struck Étienne as odd. Too simple. His instincts screamed for caution, urging him to turn back, but he had come too far to stop now. With a deep breath, he crossed the threshold and stepped into the dimly lit room.

The air was thick, stifling with an unseen presence. As Étienne moved further into the space, something caught his ear—a murmur, faint but growing louder. A low, constant whisper, like a crowd murmuring from just beyond a wall. His heart raced as he strained to listen, trying to make sense of it. It wasn't just a random sound. It felt like... voices. Dozens, maybe hundreds. The hairs on the back of his neck stood up. He could feel them—something watching him from the shadows.

He moved carefully now, his every step deliberate, his senses on high alert. His hand brushed the wall for balance, and he froze. The whispers seemed to grow, but still, there was nothing visible. He tried to steady his breathing, trying to make sense of what was happening. What had she done? What was this?

And then, he saw her.

Katya.

She was sitting at her desk, bathed in the cold glow of her computer screen, her back turned to him. She was still, her body rigid, her eyes wide open but unfocused. It was as though she hadn't noticed his presence at all. Her fingers twitched, mechanically tapping at the keyboard in a rhythm that was oddly detached from reality. She looked... wrong. Like she was no longer fully part of this world.

Étienne's pulse quickened. This wasn't the woman he had been hunting. This wasn't the person who had killed so many. This was something else entirely.

"Katya," he said, his voice calm but firm. The words

hung in the air for a moment, and for a second, he didn't think she had heard him. But then—

She turned.

Slowly. So slowly it was almost as if time itself had stretched out, distorting her movements. Her eyes locked onto his, and for a fleeting moment, Étienne thought he saw something in them. A flicker of something—otherworldly, a depth that was not human.

Her lips curved into a smile, but it was cold, almost predatory. There was no surprise in her expression, no fear. She had known he would come.

"You've been chasing me for so long, Étienne," Katya said, her voice soft and smooth, almost like a whisper from a distant dream. "But now... you've caught up."

Her words didn't feel like a confession. They didn't hold any remorse. It was as if she were simply acknowledging a truth that had been inevitable. As if she had been expecting him, welcoming him into her web of lies, power, and death.

Étienne's heart skipped a beat. Something was wrong. Something deeper than he had imagined. She wasn't afraid. There was no hint of the paranoia or fear of a cornered criminal. Katya was delighted to see him. Almost... pleased. This was not just the confrontation he had anticipated. This was a game to her.

She rose from her chair with a fluid, almost predatory grace, and as she did, Étienne felt the room shift. The air thickened, the shadows stretching around her as if they were alive. She looked at him with an almost unnatural intensity. Her eyes glowed, faintly at first, then more pronounced, the light within them shifting as though it was drawn from something deep inside her—something far darker than mere madness.

"You've come so far, but you're too late," Katya said, her

voice like velvet, smooth and hypnotic, pulling him into her orbit. She took a step toward him, her presence overwhelming, commanding the room. "You don't understand, do you? This is what I've been working for. This... is what I was born for."

Étienne stood frozen, his mind racing. What was she saying? Was she confessing to the murders? Or was there something far more terrifying at play? The voices in the room—the whispering—were growing louder now, as if they were alive, following her every word, amplifying her power. This wasn't just about murder. This was about something else. Something transcendent.

"I'm not just a murderer," Katya continued, her tone taking on an almost reverent, cult-like quality. "I am the beginning of a new world, Étienne. A world where I control life and death. Where I reshape reality itself."

The words chilled him to the bone, but it was the way she said them—like a prophet delivering a revelation—that made his blood run cold. He had thought he understood her, but now... now he saw the full scope of her delusion. She wasn't just killing people. She wasn't just committing atrocities to prove a point. She believed she was evolving—becoming something far beyond human.

Her smile widened as she stepped closer, almost gliding toward him. "Join me, Étienne," she whispered, her voice a seductive lullaby. "And you'll see. Together, we can reshape the world. We can bring it to its knees, bowing before us."

Étienne's mind reeled, but there was no time for doubt. There was no time to consider the insanity in her words. This wasn't just about bringing her to justice anymore. This was about stopping her from bringing her twisted vision to life.

The chilling realization hit him hard. She wasn't a criminal. She wasn't a killer. Katya had become something far worse: a zealot, a fanatic, a force that threatened to upend everything he understood about right and wrong.

"I'm here to stop you, Katya," Étienne said, his voice steady, even as a deep chill coursed through his veins. "This ends now."

Her response came swiftly, a low, almost mocking laugh that echoed through the room like a death knell.

"We'll see about that," she said, her eyes narrowing, the glint of power and madness dancing in them.

Étienne took a step back, but it was too late. He had walked into her domain. Now, he was her prey.

7
THE EXECUTION OF
THE PLAN

New York City - Early Spring 2020

Katya stood alone, her figure a dark silhouette against the city lights. Her apartment—bare, almost clinical in its minimalism—felt like a world apart from the chaos she was about to unleash. The city outside seemed so small now, a toy version of itself, irrelevant to the monumental shift that was about to take place. New York was just a backdrop, a fleeting distraction in her grand plan.

The view from the window was a perfect reflection of her state of mind: cold, detached, and filled with a sense of impending inevitability. The neon lights of the city flickered in the distance like distant stars, their glow harsh and unnatural. The streets below were a sea of motion, but Katya felt no connection to the life below. She was beyond them now, beyond the world of everyday struggles and concerns.

Her thoughts, like the city lights, flickered with precision. Her plan—the culmination of years of preparation—was finally in motion. The poison had been distributed. The inmates were already showing the early signs: subtle at first —weakness, dizziness, skin rashes that were easy to dismiss, even by the trained eye. It wouldn't be long before the symptoms progressed into something far worse— death. A few more hours, maybe a day at most, and her first phase would be complete. The prison system would be in chaos. Bodies would begin to pile up, their lives snuffed out like candles in a windstorm, and the authorities would be scrambling for answers they would never find.

But she was far from done. This was just the beginning.

Katya's eyes narrowed as she turned from the window and walked to her desk. The room felt suffocating as the weight of what was about to happen settled on her. She had spent years orchestrating every detail of this moment. Studying the weaknesses in the system, hacking into the food supply chains, manipulating everything from the shadows. She had built this meticulously, calculating every move, every possible outcome, until everything was ready. The death toll in the prisons was just the first ripple in a much larger, more devastating wave.

Her hands hovered over the keyboard, fingers cold and steady as she checked her laptop screen. The encrypted message was waiting for her, and her pulse quickened as she opened it. The message came from a contact deep inside the prison system—someone she had paid handsomely to ensure that everything would go according to plan.

The poison had been delivered to the largest correctional facilities in the country. It was too late for the authorities to intervene. Even if they could trace the outbreak, they wouldn't know where to start. The logistics behind the poisoning had been designed to confuse, to lead them in circles. The death count would rise, and it would be weeks—months even—before anyone could begin to piece together the truth. By the time they understood the nature of the crisis, Katya would be far beyond their reach.

Her lips curved into a smile, one that felt almost foreign to her. Power was coursing through her veins now. Every death, every soul lost, would bring her closer to what she truly believed was her rightful place in the world. She was no longer bound by the limits of humanity. She was transcending—becoming something greater. And as the souls of the dead joined her, as they sought her out in their final moments, she would become a queen in a realm of her own making. The deaths would become a sacred rite, a cleansing of the corrupt, a purification. The souls of the departed would kneel at her feet, and she would take her place among them, ruling over life and death itself.

Her breathing grew slow, methodical, as if she could almost feel the spiritual energy of the souls that would soon converge with her own. The world she was creating was inevitable. There was no turning back. And yet, a small part of her—a small, almost insignificant part—wondered how she would be remembered. Would history see her as a visionary? A divine force? Or would they call her a monster?

She didn't care. They would never understand.

As her thoughts swirled, a sudden knock at the door shattered the silence.

Her hand froze mid-air, fingers hovering over the keyboard. Who could it be? The timing seemed off—too soon, too precise. She had made sure that no one knew she was here. No one could find her. But this—this was different. She had been expecting the world to come to her, but this was an interruption she hadn't planned for.

The knock came again, more urgent this time. Whoever it was, they were determined to get her attention.

A flicker of unease passed through her. It wasn't fear—she had long ago learned to disregard such emotions—but a momentary crack in her carefully crafted façade. Katya straightened, her eyes narrowing as she turned away from the screen and toward the door.

Was this the moment the world would catch up to her? Was someone finally about to expose her, to end her reign before it could fully begin?

No, she couldn't afford to let anything—anyone—distract her now. There was too much at stake.

With deliberate calm, she crossed the room toward the door. Each step was measured, her thoughts already shifting to her next move. If someone had found her, they wouldn't get away so easily. After all, she had prepared for everything.

Her fingers brushed the cool metal of the doorknob, and for just a moment, she allowed herself a small smile. Whatever this was, it wouldn't stop her. Not now. Not when she was so close.

She opened the door, fully prepared for whatever—or whoever—was on the other side.

Étienne's Pursuit

Étienne had spent days chasing every lead, every thread, and the closer he got to Katya, the more suffocating the truth became. The pieces of the puzzle were finally falling into place, but they felt disjointed, out of sync—like a broken mosaic that refused to reveal a clear picture. With every step, he uncovered another layer of deception, another part of her plan he hadn't foreseen. What had begun as an investigation into a series of suspicious deaths linked to food poisoning had transformed into something far darker. This was no longer just about tainted food or missing prisoners. This was about total domination, manipulation on a global scale, the calculated destruction of everything—institutions, systems, even the very fabric of human morality.

Katya wasn't just some lone killer with a twisted agenda. She was a mastermind, a force that had orchestrated an entire web of chaos and deception, each strand woven so tightly that it would be impossible to untangle without destroying everything in its path. Étienne had uncovered her fingerprints on every corner of this nightmare: from the underground network of corrupt officials to the high-tech hacks into the prison food suppliers and government contracts. She was everywhere. Her influence seeped into every crevice of the world, manipulating everyone and everything in her reach.

And through it all, Étienne knew one thing for sure: Katya was not just a murderer. She was something darker, something far more dangerous—a person who viewed herself not as a villain, but as a visionary.

He had finally tracked her down to her apartment—a place he knew was going to be more than just a hideout. It was a symbol of her control, of the power she had already claimed. When he stepped inside, the atmosphere felt heavy. The air was thick, pregnant with the weight of her presence. It was almost as if the walls themselves had been imbued with her will. Every inch of the apartment seemed deliberately chosen, its cold, minimalist décor somehow reflecting her personality: stark, efficient, impersonal. It was a place where thoughts dominated, where emotions took a back seat. There was no warmth here—only a deep, unsettling stillness.

And then he saw her.

There she was, sitting by the window, staring out at the sprawling city below. She didn't even flinch when he entered the room, didn't acknowledge his presence. Was she waiting for him? Had she known all along that he would come? He wasn't sure. But that thought made the hair on the back of his neck stand up. She wasn't surprised to see him, and she wasn't scared. That realization hit him harder than any physical blow.

"Katya," Étienne said, his voice steady, though his heart was pounding in his chest. He could feel the weight of the moment pressing down on him. This wasn't just another interview or conversation. This was the endgame. There was no more running, no more subterfuge. This was the confrontation he had been anticipating, the moment when everything he had learned would either be confirmed or shattered.

Slowly, she turned to face him, and her smile was like a predator's. Slow, deliberate, almost knowing—as if she already knew how this would play out. "I knew you'd come," she said, her voice soft but filled with an unsettling calm. "You always do, don't you, Étienne? You never stop chasing. You never stop digging for the truth."

She wasn't wrong. Étienne had always pursued the truth with an almost obsessive determination. But this wasn't just about uncovering a story. This was about survival. This was about stopping her before she could create something far worse than he had ever imagined.

He clenched his fists, his anger bubbling to the surface. "You're a monster," he spat, the words coming out harsher than he intended. The disgust in his voice was clear. He wanted her to hear it. To feel the weight of what she had done, what she was continuing to do.

Katya didn't flinch. She stood up, her movements fluid, almost graceful—as if she were floating. She walked toward him with an air of calm superiority, her eyes unwavering. Serene. Divine, even.

"I'm not a monster," she said, her voice gentle yet firm, as though trying to soothe a child. "I'm a visionary. I'm offering the world something it's never had before. Control. Power. Immortality. Do you understand, Étienne? I'm giving them everything they've ever dreamed of."

Étienne's stomach churned. Control. Power. Immortality. The words felt like poison, the ideology behind them twisted and sickening. She wasn't trying to save anyone. She was trying to dominate them—reshape them into a world where she was a goddess, a ruler over life and death. That was her vision.

"You're delusional," Étienne shot back, his voice rising in frustration. "You've convinced yourself that murdering people is some kind of... divine act. But you're just a murderer, Katya. A psychopath. And I'm going to stop you."

Her laugh interrupted him. It was light and airy, almost like a prayer being whispered. It was unsettling—too serene, too calm for the words she was speaking. Hypnotic. "You think I'm a psychopath? I'm beyond that, Étienne. I've ascended. You'll understand soon enough. You've been chasing shadows, trying to make sense of something that you'll never fully grasp."

Her words twisted inside him. She wasn't just acknowledging her crimes; she was celebrating them. To her, the deaths were a necessary sacrifice—each life lost, each soul claimed, was a step closer to her ascension.

"But I'm giving you the opportunity to join me," she

continued, her tone almost tender. "Together, we can reshape the world. You and I. You're the perfect partner for this."

Étienne's resolve hardened. She wanted him on her side. She didn't understand. She couldn't understand. This wasn't some philosophical debate. This was about stopping her—before she could turn her twisted vision into a living nightmare.

"I'll never join you," he said, his words sharp, cutting through the tension like a knife.

Her smile deepened, almost sympathetic. It was a smile that spoke of someone who truly believed in her own divine purpose, someone who knew that she was right. "That's a shame. Because in the end, Étienne, you'll realize I was right all along. But it won't matter then. By then, you'll be just like them—dead."

The air in the room seemed to crackle with tension. Katya had already decided her fate. Her vision was too strong, too overwhelming for her to reconsider. She wasn't just a woman—she was a force, and Étienne was merely a bystander in the story she had written.

But Étienne was determined. He wouldn't be her puppet. Not now. Not ever.

This was no longer just a matter of exposing the truth. This was about stopping the apocalypse she was planning.

The Poison Takes Hold

The poison had spread with a terrifying swiftness across the U.S. prison system, and the authorities were struggling to keep up. The initial reports were fragmented, scattered, as if the entire country was holding its breath, waiting for the full scope of the disaster to emerge. But each report only added to the confusion. What had started as a handful of inexplicable deaths quickly escalated into an all-out crisis. The prisons, already overcrowded and under-funded, had become ground zero for an unprecedented outbreak.

The first few deaths were difficult to track. Prisoners had collapsed unexpectedly, some barely showing any signs of illness before they died. Others fell ill, but their symptoms were unlike anything the medical staff had ever encountered. There were no clear patterns—some of the inmates dropped dead within a matter of hours, their bodies succumbing to some unseen force. Others lingered for days, their condition deteriorating slowly, painfully. They experienced a bizarre progression: first, a light dizziness, then rashes that spread rapidly across their bodies, followed by extreme weakness, and finally, delirium. By the time they reached the final stages, they were almost unrecognizable—pale, disoriented, gasping for breath, as if their bodies were no longer their own.

The poison seemed to adapt to each individual, mutating, changing, finding new ways to incapacitate its victims. The authorities were baffled. The CDC had dispatched a team of highly trained experts, but their findings were inconclusive. The typical tests for toxins, poisons, and biological agents came back empty. Nothing matched. The toxins didn't show up on any known tests. There were no traces of typical poisons like cyanide or ricin, and the symptoms didn't fit any known viruses or bacteria. The only thing everyone could agree on was that this wasn't any kind of natural outbreak. It was deliberate.

Still, the authorities struggled to comprehend the scope of the epidemic. Inmates were dropping like flies—a term that had once seemed exaggerated, but now felt disturbingly accurate. They were dying too quickly, and too unpredictably. The disease's strange progression baffled doctors and overwhelmed the prison system. What made matters worse was the chaos inside the prisons. Prison guards were getting sick too, stricken with the same mysterious symptoms as the inmates. Those who managed to stay healthy were too overwhelmed to contain the rioting that had broken out. Fear and confusion spread like wildfire, as disoriented, panicked inmates clashed with guards, some attacking anyone within reach in a desperate bid for escape. Others barricaded themselves in their cells, paralyzed by the terror of not knowing whether they would live or die.

At Rikers Island, one of the largest and most notorious prisons, the situation was especially grim. The prison descended into chaos. Guards, who were already stretched thin, couldn't keep up with the unrest. Inmates, terrified and confused, began fighting amongst themselves, as if the threat of death had already begun to shatter their collective sanity. The worst part? No one had any answers. No one knew what was causing the deaths, and no one had a solution to stop it. The hospital units were filled to capacity, with people too sick to be treated. The entire facility seemed to be on the verge of total collapse.

While the world outside struggled to grasp what was unfolding, Katya remained at the heart of it all, observing from the safety of her New York apartment. Her face was serene, almost detached, as she gazed out at the city skyline. The lights below flickered, as if the world itself were trembling under the weight of the chaos she had set in motion. She raised a glass of wine to her lips, savoring the taste, before turning her attention back to the screen of her laptop, where live updates of the spreading epidemic flashed before her eyes.

The poison was her design, her creation. Every death, every symptom, every moment of confusion and fear—Katya was behind it all. She wasn't just an observer. She was the architect of the crisis. Each life lost, each soul claimed, brought her closer to something she had been working toward for years. She was mastering death, one person at a time. It was all falling into place.

And she revelled in it.

Every moment of panic unfolding before her eyes felt like a personal triumph. The hospitals were overwhelmed. The authorities were scrambling. The news media was already spinning out of control, speculating about bioterrorism, a rogue killer, or even a new viral plague. None of them had a clue. They were all playing into her hands. Katya had expected this. She had planned for it. The media frenzy, the misinformation—it was all part of the show. This was her grand experiment, and now it was in full motion.

Katya felt the power coursing through her veins, stronger than ever before. The souls of the dead were already gathering around her, their whispers filling the empty spaces of her mind. They were her followers now, her loyal subjects, guiding her toward the next step. The more death she caused, the more powerful she became. She could already feel herself evolving, transcending the limitations of human existence. She was no longer bound by the rules of morality, or even by life and death. She was something greater, something unstoppable.

She glanced once more at the reports flooding in—Rikers Island, death toll rising, hospitals overwhelmed, authorities unable to track down the source. It was just the beginning. This was her moment. And with every passing second, as the world descended into chaos, Katya's vision for the future grew clearer. She would reshape the world from the ground up. And the world would bow to her.

But this was only the first phase.

As the poison spread, as the riots escalated, and the death toll climbed, Katya knew it was just a matter of time before the world would be hers. And nothing—not Étienne, not the authorities, not the chaos she had unleashed—could stop her now.

The Showdown

The tension in the air was palpable as Étienne and Katya faced each other, the weight of everything they had been through—every lie, every death, every misstep—finally coming to a head. Étienne's heart hammered in his chest. He could feel the gravity of the moment. This wasn't just an investigation anymore. This was a confrontation. A fight for the future, and he was prepared to do whatever it took to stop her.

He took a step forward, each movement deliberate, his eyes locked on her with unflinching resolve. "You've crossed the line, Katya. This isn't some sick fantasy you've created. People are dying, real people—people with families, lives. And for what? So you can feel like a god?"

His words hung heavy in the air, accusatory, full of a righteous anger that had been building for weeks. His mind raced back to the countless victims, to the prison outbreaks, the senseless chaos she had unleashed. How many had died because of her? How many families had been torn apart? And for what? All of this, just for the satisfaction of her delusional ambitions. He couldn't let her succeed. He wouldn't let her become the monster she wanted to be.

Katya's response came slowly, almost too calm for the gravity of the moment. Instead of lashing out or defending herself, she stepped closer to him, as if drawn by some invisible force. Her gaze was intense, almost hypnotic, her eyes never leaving his, as though she was trying to reach into his very soul. The quiet intensity of her presence sent a chill down his spine.

"You don't understand, Étienne. The dead... they whisper to me. They guide me. Every soul I claim adds to my power. I've been chosen," she said, her voice soft but steady, as though the words were part of a mantra she had said a thousand times. "You could be too, if you stopped fighting it."

Her words were mesmerizing, but Étienne didn't falter. He was no stranger to her manipulation, her twisted vision. He had seen it all. He had followed the trail of bodies, of lies, of chaos she had left in her wake. It was clear now: this wasn't about power, or control, or the deaths themselves. It was about self-deification, about her belief that she was somehow divinely chosen. She had become so consumed by her own narrative that she couldn't even see the destruction she had caused.

"I'll stop you," Étienne said, his voice low, but full of resolve. His fists clenched at his sides. He didn't care about her power, her delusions. All that mattered now was stopping her, no matter the cost.

Katya's smile faded, and her face seemed to shift. The calm, almost ethereal quality of her presence suddenly hardened into something darker, more calculated. Her eyes narrowed, and her lips curled into a tight, knowing grin. "I don't think you can," she said, her words slow, deliberate, as if savoring the inevitability of it all.

Before Étienne could respond, the sudden buzz of her phone shattered the tension. It was a sound that seemed almost out of place in the charged atmosphere. Katya glanced down at the screen, her expression shifting in a fraction of a second. Her eyes narrowed as she read the message, a flicker of concern flashing across her face.

For a moment, she seemed almost human again, as if the weight of something beyond her control had interrupted her vision of divine grandeur. The first phase of her plan had gone off without a hitch, but something had changed. Her contact within the prison system had gone dark. The authorities were starting to connect the dots. It was only a matter of time before the full scale of the poisonings became known, and her carefully orchestrated scheme was exposed. The thought seemed to disturb her, but only for an instant.

Katya didn't waste another second. Her gaze flickered back to Étienne, her face hardening into something unreadable, before she moved with an unnerving swiftness. She crossed the room before Étienne could react, and the space between them seemed to shrink, the room feeling smaller, claustrophobic, as if the walls were closing in. Every step she took felt like a commanding presence, each movement a step toward sealing her vision of the future.

She leaned in close to him, so close he could feel the coolness of her breath against his skin. "You're not going to stop me, Étienne," she said, her voice soft but chilling, as though she was speaking to him from a great distance, from some higher plane of existence. "I've already won. I've already become something greater than you could ever imagine."

It wasn't a threat. It was a statement of fact. In her mind, there was no room for doubt. She had already ascended, already become something beyond human comprehension. To her, Étienne was just another obstacle, another soul who could either submit to her will or be swept aside in the wake of her unstoppable force.

She turned then, and for a moment, Étienne was sure she was going to walk away—just like that. Leave him standing there in the shadow of her victory. "Goodbye, Étienne. I'm sorry it had to be this way," she said, almost as if the apology was an afterthought.

The door clicked shut behind her with a finality that echoed in Étienne's chest, and for a heartbeat, the world seemed to freeze.

He stood frozen for a moment, his mind racing. She was unstoppable—not just because of her intellect, her strategic genius, or her ability to manipulate systems. No, she was unstoppable because she had convinced herself that she was meant to win, that the world had no choice but to bend to her vision. And that kind of belief, that kind of delusion, made her more dangerous than anything he had ever faced.

Étienne's fists tightened, his breath coming out in shallow bursts as the realization set in. He had thought he could stop her, confront her with logic, with facts, but he had underestimated her. Her power wasn't just in her intellect—it was in her conviction, her obsession with her own divinity.

But Étienne didn't have the luxury of doubt. He couldn't let her win. He couldn't let her become the monster she believed she was destined to be.

He turned on his heel, his heart pounding in his chest.

There was still time. There had to be. He wasn't done yet. Not by a long shot.

8

THE AFTERMATH

New York City - Mid-Spring 2020
The city pulsed with a frantic, almost chaotic energy, as the magnitude of the crisis unfolded. The streets buzzed with the usual hustle and bustle, but there was an undercurrent of tension in the air, as if the very fabric of New York had been disrupted. Sirens blared in the distance. Ambulances sped through intersections, barely slowing down as they passed. Every news outlet seemed to be running the same headline—"Unexplained Deaths Rip Through U.S. Prisons"—but no one had yet pieced together the horrific truth that was lurking beneath the surface. The poisonings were happening on a scale far larger than anyone could imagine. And the authorities, despite their best efforts, were blind to the true mastermind behind it all.

Étienne could feel the weight of it. The tension was palpable, and as he stood there, outside the government building, his phone buzzing in his hand, a sick feeling settled in his gut. He swiped across the screen, scrolling through the latest updates on the tragedy:

"Poisoning Deaths Across the U.S. Prison System Continue to Rise; Authorities Are Stumped."

Each word seemed to cut deeper into him. He had known this was coming—the inevitable escalation of the poisonings—but seeing the headline, seeing the panic begin to take hold of the nation, made it all too real. The crisis was unfolding before his eyes, and Katya was at the center of it, pulling the strings with devastating precision.

Étienne's fingers trembled slightly as he read the article. The numbers were staggering, but what unsettled him even more was how everyone had failed to make the connection. The deaths, the symptoms—they were all linked to the food supply system, to the prisons. But no one had tied it to the woman who had been at the heart of everything. To Katya.

Her plan had worked flawlessly—at least, on the surface. The authorities were still in the dark, scrambling to understand the scope of the deaths, trying to locate the source of the poison. But by the time they figured it out, it would already be too late. She had already vanished into the shadows, leaving nothing but confusion and death in her wake.

Étienne felt the sinking weight of failure wash over him. This had been his pursuit for weeks, for months now, and yet, somehow, he had been outmaneuvered at every turn. Every lead, every piece of information, had been carefully orchestrated by Katya. The false trails. The misdirections. The poisoned food chain that had been spread across the entire prison system. She had played him from the beginning, and now the damage was done.

He looked up at the government building before him, its imposing structure a stark reminder of the system he had been working so hard to expose. But the more he looked at it, the more it seemed like part of the problem. The bureaucracy, the red tape, the blind spots in the investigation—they had all allowed this to happen. They had allowed Katya to operate under their radar, to wreak havoc with nothing but the flicker of a keystroke and a poison in the food supply. It was the perfect crime—a crime that no one had seen coming, and no one could stop.

His phone buzzed again, this time with a message from Claire. Her words were blunt:

"It's over, Étienne. She's already won."

He stared at the screen for a moment, feeling the sting of her words hit harder than he expected. Claire had been the one person who had stuck by him through the investigation, who had believed in his ability to bring Katya down. But now, even she seemed to have given up. The reality was clear: he had failed.

The chaos was spreading faster than anyone could contain it. Prisons were on lockdown, but the outbreaks were multiplying, and the media frenzy was only adding fuel to the fire. People were beginning to panic. Rumors swirled that the poison had been deliberately spread. That it was targeting the most vulnerable. That it was connected to some kind of mysterious force. And as the death toll rose, so did the fear, the paranoia, and the loss of control.

Étienne had tried to be the one to uncover the truth, to expose Katya and bring her to justice. But now, as he stood there outside the building, he realized that the damage had already been done. The world was changing, and the shadows that Katya had cast were only growing longer.

A cold breeze ruffled his coat as he stood in the street, the noise of the city muffled in his ears. His body felt heavy, as if the weight of everything was pulling him down. There was no escaping the truth now. Katya had won.

But even as the realization set in, a small spark of defiance ignited in Étienne's chest. No, he hadn't stopped her, not yet. The world might be reeling, but there was still time. Katya wasn't invincible. She had made mistakes, left traces behind. If he could just follow the thread, if he could piece it all together, there was still a chance to stop her.

Étienne's gaze hardened as he slid the phone back into his pocket. He wasn't done yet. Not by a long shot.

He turned and walked back toward the chaos, his footsteps resolute. The world had gone mad, but he wasn't giving up. Not yet. The truth was still out there. And he would find it, no matter the cost.

Katya's Victory

In the stillness of her apartment, Katya sat on the floor, her back pressed against the cold, brick wall, her legs crossed in a meditative posture. The city outside continued to pulse with life, but inside, there was only an overwhelming peace. For the first time in years, her mind was clear, her body calm, and her heart steady. The weight of the chaos she had orchestrated, the destruction she had unleashed, no longer burdened her. In fact, it felt like a distant memory, a phase in her evolution that had already passed.

Her victory was tangible now. The deaths, the poisonings, the destruction of the prison system, all of it had been part of a greater design. Every soul that had passed into the afterlife was not just a loss—it was a sacrifice, one that had elevated her. As the architect of their deaths, she had moved beyond the realm of mere mortals. The souls of the deceased swirled around her like whispers, murmurs of adoration and reverence, guiding her, filling her with an unearthly power. She was untouchable, beyond the reach of any law, any mortal justice. She was the next step in human evolution—a being who commanded not just life and death, but the very essence of the universe itself.

The stillness was broken by the soft vibration of her phone on the table, an almost imperceptible buzz that seemed to reverberate through the silence. Katya opened her eyes, the calm never leaving her face. She knew who it was before she even looked. Claire.

Claire had been her ally, her confidante throughout the entire journey. The one person who understood her vision, who stood with her as she toppled systems of power. And now, her message confirmed that the final phase of Katya's plan was unfolding just as she had imagined.

She reached for the phone, her fingers dancing across the screen as she read Claire's message. The words were brief, but they carried the weight of everything that had been building up. "Katya... it's time."

Katya allowed herself a small, knowing smile. It was time. The world outside had been consumed with confusion and fear, but she was no longer playing the game of chaos for chaos's sake. Her vision had already been realized. She had proven her power. The souls of the dead had joined her. They had ascended alongside her, and now the world was on the verge of collapse. But that collapse was not her end. It was only the beginning. The true test had yet to come.

She was done with death, at least for the time being. The bloodshed was necessary for her to break free—but the next step was far greater. She would lead. She would be the one the world turned to in its hour of need. They would come to her, begging for salvation, for guidance, for a new world order.

They would bow before her vision, and she would give them everything they needed to believe in her: control. She had already shown them what she was capable of, and now, she would show them what a true goddess could do with the power of life and death at her fingertips. The world would collapse into chaos, yes, but Katya would be there to rebuild it—her way.

Her mind raced ahead, imagining the world, restructured in her image. She could feel the ripples of change already beginning to ripple through the air. Nothing would stop her now. The foundations of society, the very structures of power, were crumbling under the weight of her influence, and the world was on the brink of transformation.

But then, as if to remind her that not everything was within her control, her phone buzzed again. This time, the screen displayed an incoming call. Katya's eyes narrowed with curiosity as she saw the name flashing across the display. Étienne.

The name sent a small jolt of recognition through her. He had been the one constant thorn in her side, the one person who had never stopped chasing her, never stopped trying to expose her. She hadn't expected him to still be in the picture—not after everything. But now, it seemed, he was reaching out to her.

Her smile didn't waver as she answered the call. There was something almost familiar in the way he'd always challenged her, something that made him an ideal opponent. But now, it was too late. She had already won. And this final confrontation, whatever it was, would only serve to prove that he was too far behind.

"Katya," Étienne's voice came through the phone. His tone was calm, yet there was an undercurrent of something darker, something heavier that gave her pause for a moment. He knew, perhaps, that he was too late. He knew that the world was already changing, but she couldn't help the small thrill of hearing his voice again, his words now tinged with a sense of finality.

She leaned back against the wall again, closing her eyes for a moment as she let the moment linger. Then she responded, her voice soft, almost affectionate, as if speaking to a lost soul.

"I'm glad you've finally decided to speak to me, Étienne." Her voice was smooth, laced with a quiet power. "I thought you might try to stop me, but now… now you see." She didn't need to elaborate. The truth was obvious. He had been chasing shadows for far too long, chasing her with a purpose that had become meaningless in the face of the truth.

"I see everything," Étienne's voice came again, but this time there was something colder in it, something that sent a shiver through her. "And so will the world."

Her smile only deepened, a small, knowing grin that spoke of everything she had become. It was too late. Even Étienne, despite his best efforts, couldn't stop what had already been set in motion. The world was about to learn what she had known all along: she was not just a woman. She was something more. She was a force of nature.

Katya let the silence stretch between them, feeling the weight of her victory settle over her like a warm cloak. No more games. No more false pretenses. She had reached the pinnacle, and nothing—no one—could stop her now.

"Goodbye, Étienne." The words were almost tender, spoken with the quiet certainty of a woman who had already transcended the world as it was. "I'm sorry it had to be this way." Then, she hung up. The victory was hers.

. . .

Étienne's Dilemma

Étienne walked through the sleek, sterile hallways of the FBI headquarters in Washington, but it felt as if he were walking through a fog, the weight of his thoughts clouding his mind. He was in a building designed for action, a place where decisions were made and the forces of law and order converged. But today, it felt like nothing more than a mausoleum—a place where all the evidence that should have led to justice only seemed to confirm one thing: Katya had already won.

Every step he took echoed in the hallway, each one amplifying the growing sense of helplessness that gnawed at him. His fingers brushed the edges of the files he was carrying, their weight no longer just physical, but symbolic. They were filled with hard evidence: financial records, encrypted communications, cell phone data, and witness testimony. Everything pointed back to Katya—every poisoned prison, every misdirected lead, every digital trail that had led him through a labyrinth of deception. Her influence had been woven so intricately into every layer of the world around him that there was no way to untangle it now. She had orchestrated it all.

But that wasn't the most chilling part. As he sat down at his desk, the files spread out before him like the pieces of an unholy puzzle, he realized something far more sinister. Katya wasn't just a mastermind killer. She had transcended her role as a mere criminal. She had become an idea—a symbol. She wasn't just someone he could expose or stop. No, she was the movement now. A force of nature.

His mind kept returning to the reports he'd read, the whispers that had begun to spread through the public.

Katya wasn't just being feared; she was being worshipped. Her social media presence—those cryptic posts that had once seemed like the ramblings of a deranged mind—had now become gospel to a growing legion of followers. People, desperate for meaning, were being drawn into her vision. The stories of her ascension, of her belief that she was becoming something greater than human, were no longer dismissed as the rantings of a madwoman. They were being shared. Reposted. She was promising her followers not just death but immortality, a place in a new order where control and power over life and death were hers to command. The illusion had become a reality for them. And more frighteningly, people were buying into it.

The idea of Katya had transformed. She wasn't just a killer anymore. She had turned into a prophet, a goddess-like figure with the promise of reshaping the world. Her voice was no longer one of a criminal; it was that of someone who could change reality itself. And now, instead of trying to stop her, Étienne found himself facing a new kind of enemy—one that didn't simply defy the law, but one who had successfully rewritten the rules of how the world saw power and control.

Could he stop her now?

The question reverberated in his mind like a drumbeat, each time louder than the last. The evidence was right in front of him, undeniable. But it felt like he was fighting a shadow—a figment of something much greater. Katya had become so much more than a woman in the shadows, pulling strings. She had harnessed the collective fear, the uncertainty, and the raw hunger for something more that plagued so many. Her promises were intoxicating. And as Étienne watched the news cycle, he saw what he feared most: People weren't just terrified of her. They were beginning to believe her.

The public perception of Katya had shifted. No longer was she the faceless villain behind the poisonings. She was becoming a revolutionary figure, a martyr to those who had felt lost or broken by society. She was the savior they never knew they needed. In her followers' eyes, she had become invincible. And to them, the ends justified the means. They didn't care about the lives she had destroyed. They cared about the new world she promised—one where they had a place of power and purpose. She was the leader they had been waiting for.

Étienne stared at the screen in front of him, the evidence spread before him like a graveyard of failed attempts, each one revealing just how far-reaching Katya's influence had become. He had chased the wrong leads, fallen into her traps, and now it was clear: Katya's plan wasn't just about destruction—it was about revolution. Control. She had become a force beyond anything Étienne had imagined. And it terrified him to think that, in some twisted way, she might actually be right.

The realization hit him with the force of a physical blow: Katya had already won.

She had created something so powerful, so seductive, that it was out of his reach now. People weren't just following her orders—they were following her vision. They were ready to build a new world, not just destroy the old one. And in doing so, they had given her the power she needed to become something immortal. Even if Étienne exposed her, it wouldn't matter. The movement was already too big. She was no longer a criminal—it was her vision that had taken root in the hearts and minds of so many.

But Étienne wasn't ready to give up. He couldn't let it end like this. Not after everything. He wasn't prepared to accept that this woman, this monster, would be remembered as the one who changed the world. He had a duty—not just to the truth, but to the people who had been drawn into her orbit. To the ones who still hadn't been recruited yet, to the innocent who didn't know what they were walking into.

For Étienne, it wasn't about justice anymore. It was about fighting the tide, even if he couldn't win. He couldn't let her become the leader of this new world order, the symbol of what was coming. He wasn't ready to see everything he fought for crumble into her hands.

The only thing Étienne knew for certain as he sat at his desk, lost in his thoughts, was this: The battle was far from over. He would keep fighting, even if the whole world had turned its back on him. He had to stop her—for the world, and for the people still lost in her dangerous grip.

And with that thought, Étienne made a decision. The stakes were higher than ever. This wasn't just about catching a killer anymore—it was about saving a world that had already begun to crumble under Katya's influence.

Katya's Delusions Unravel

Katya's phone call with Étienne had ended, and for a moment, she simply sat there in the silence of her apartment, the weight of the conversation still hanging in the air. The faint hum of the city outside her window seemed distant, but the sirens in the background echoed like the beat of her own fractured mind. She closed her eyes for a moment, absorbing the sound of the world's chaos—chaos that, in her mind, she had orchestrated, controlled, and now reigned over.

But as she sat there, contemplating her next move, a fleeting doubt crept in. Étienne's words, calm and pointed, lingered in her thoughts. "I see everything," he had said. His voice hadn't wavered; it had been calm, but it had carried an undeniable weight—an undercurrent of finality. The stark truth of what he had said had started to settle, digging beneath her layered confidence, forcing her to ask: *Was she truly becoming what she believed herself to be?* A god?

For a moment, that thought caught her off-guard. She'd spent years crafting this illusion of divinity. She had spent sleepless nights envisioning a world where she reigned supreme, where she could wield life and death like a puppet master, where those who opposed her would either kneel before her or be wiped out. Her actions had been justified in her own mind, each life taken as a sacrifice toward her ultimate goal—godhood. She had purged the world of its filth, elevated herself above it, and now, in her mind, she controlled everything.

But now, as she sat in the shadowed room, the world outside stretching endlessly, chaotic and beyond her control, that certainty began to slip. Was she truly the one orchestrating it all? Or had she become the pawn in her own twisted game?

With a sharp breath, Katya quickly dismissed the thought. She couldn't afford to entertain it. Her vision was too close, the power she sought too within reach. She had taken control—she had dictated the course of events. The media was already playing her game, glorifying her as something greater, a revolutionary who could rid the world of its rotting core. Dictators had done it before, tyrants had risen from the bloodshed of millions, and she would rise from the ashes of this world as they had. They would come to her. They would bow to her.

She was unstoppable.

But as she looked around the sterile, darkened apartment, a creeping sense of unease began to take hold. The silence of the room, the stillness of everything around her—it was suffocating. The walls, once a refuge for her in her pursuit of power, now seemed to close in. The weight of it all, the responsibility, the sin, the lives she had taken—every little piece of her grand design—it all seemed to push down on her chest, too heavy to carry.

Her hands trembled slightly as she reached for the glass of wine on the nearby table, the liquid feeling more like poison than a luxury drink now. She took a long sip, but it offered no comfort. Instead, the taste felt bitter, like ashes in her mouth. She glanced around, half-expecting the whispers of the dead to console her, to remind her of the souls she had claimed—the ones that had, in her mind, elevated her, empowered her. They had been her guides, her followers, and they had given her strength. But now, their voices seemed different—no longer a source of reassurance.

The whispers had changed.

They no longer felt like a source of divine power, but like a chorus of lamentations, a sea of souls trapped in a web they couldn't escape. They were not her guides anymore. They were her burden. The weight of their ghostly presence pressing down on her shoulders was overwhelming, suffocating, until she could barely breathe. What had once been a warm, comforting embrace now felt like an anchor that threatened to pull her under.

She could hear their voices, each one more fragmented than the last. They were no longer offering guidance or praise, but demanding something from her—something she wasn't sure she could give. The words in the dark seemed to meld with her own thoughts, twisting into an eerie cacophony that gnawed at her mind.

"More... more... you must do more."

"The price is coming... the price of your victory."

Victory. The word echoed through her mind, but it no longer felt like the sweet triumph she had anticipated. There was something darker, more costly about it now. The delusions that had sustained her for so long were now beginning to crack, revealing the truth behind her illusion of control. She had thought she was ascending, but now, in the quiet of the room, the truth seemed unavoidable: Her victory had come at a cost, and she could feel that cost in her bones, like a weight she couldn't escape.

The weight of the souls she had claimed was becoming too much to bear. Every life lost felt like a chain around her neck, tightening with each passing hour. She could feel them now, those she had taken—their angry whispers, their demands for release, their remorse. And it terrified her. Had she really become something greater, or had she merely become a prisoner of her own making?

She pressed her hands to her ears, but the voices only grew louder, as if the spirits she had thought to control were now controlling her. There was no escape. She could feel the weight of every death, every action, bearing down on her, crushing her spirit.

For the first time since she had begun her descent into madness, she felt the true cost of what she had done. She had imagined that when she reached her godlike ascension, everything would fall into place. But what if, instead of ascension, this was the descent into something much darker? What if, instead of being elevated, she was being consumed by the very power she had sought to control?

Her phone buzzed again, pulling her from her thoughts. She glanced at the screen—another message. But the message didn't matter anymore. Nothing mattered except the feeling of emptiness settling in her chest, the realization that the victory she had so long dreamed of had turned into an endless, gnawing burden.

Katya had become something she couldn't even recognize. The cracks in her delusion had finally opened wide enough to let the truth in, and now it was too late to turn back.

Étienne's Reflection

Étienne stood motionless at the window of his hotel room, his gaze cast over the sprawling, frenetic city below. The lights of New York City blinked like fleeting stars, indifferent to the chaos unfolding just beneath their glow. The city seemed so alive, so full of potential—but for Étienne, it felt like a hollow place. Everything had been tainted by his pursuit of Katya. The investigation had consumed him, gnawing at his soul until there was little left.

The reflection of his worn face in the window was a stark contrast to the vibrant cityscape outside. The harsh lines beneath his eyes, the slouched shoulders, the slow, measured way he moved—he didn't look like the man who had once set out to bring justice. He looked like someone who had been broken, whose very essence had been siphoned by the darkness he had chased for so long. Katya's madness hadn't just infected her world—it had invaded his, become a stain on everything he held dear. Her chaos had seeped into him like a poison, making everything seem meaningless.

He turned away from the window and glanced down at

his phone, where a photo of his sister, Clair, stared back at him. It was a reminder of everything he had lost—the person he was supposed to protect, the love he was supposed to carry through everything. The memory of Claire had kept him grounded when everything else felt like it was slipping through his fingers. And yet, now, her face seemed like a distant echo, like something he was striving to save, but in reality, something that had already been lost in his mind.

He ran his hand over his face, feeling the weight of his own failure settling on him like a dark cloud. Could he ever forgive himself? The question gnawed at him, relentless and unforgiving. He had failed. He had spent months—years—chasing Katya through every lead, every trail, and he had still come up short. The destruction she had caused had been so far-reaching, so precise, that even now, as he stood there, he could feel the ripples of her influence. How could he face the truth that he had been unable to stop her before she had spread her madness to so many?

The thought that Katya had already become something more than just a murderer, something more like an idea, a vision, only made it harder to bear. Her delusions of godhood had taken root in a way Étienne had never expected. She wasn't just a killer anymore—she was a movement, a prophet in the eyes of the people she had corrupted. The implications were terrifying. She had infected the very minds of those who followed her, planting seeds of chaos that could blossom into something much worse than anything he could have imagined. It was as though the madness was contagious, spreading through every corner of society. She had turned herself into an idea, and no one was prepared to fight an idea.

Étienne's fingers tightened around his phone as he

turned it over in his hand. He glanced at the time—a reminder that the endgame was now upon them. The authorities were closing in on her. Katya's carefully constructed empire of lies and death would eventually crumble. Her own delusions would carry her too far, and in the end, she would slip up, and they would catch her. It was just a matter of time before she made a mistake, before her grand vision unraveled. But even as that thought passed through his mind, Étienne couldn't shake the unease that lingered in his chest. Katya had already won something irreversible. The seed she had planted was already taking root, and that was the part he feared most.

He had to stay close. He had to keep fighting. Even if it felt like an impossible battle, he couldn't let go. He couldn't give up. It was the only thing that kept him grounded now —the knowledge that he might be the only one left who could prevent Katya from dragging the world down into the abyss she had created. Her story, he knew, would eventually come to an end, like all tales of madness. But the damage she had inflicted—the fractures she had caused in the world—might never heal.

Étienne took a deep breath, his mind momentarily clearing as he thought of Claire, of everything he had lost, of everything he had sacrificed to bring justice. The thought of her face, her voice, kept him rooted in the fight. He couldn't give up now, even if it felt like she had already won. He owed it to the people still out there, the ones still vulnerable to Katya's madness, to keep pushing forward.

No one could claim godhood by killing others, no matter how much they believed it. Her story would end, and when it did, Étienne would be there. He would be there to ensure that it didn't end with her victory. He had to be there when the madness collapsed—to make sure that when the world finally recognized her for what she truly was, it wouldn't be too late for anyone else.

The Final Reflection

The world outside Katya's apartment had descended into utter chaos. The air was thick with fear and uncertainty. People whispered in hushed tones about the mysterious deaths that had swept through the prison systems, about the strange illnesses that had plagued the population, about the unsettling rise of a figure who was slowly becoming more than just a criminal—she was becoming a myth. Governments were scrambling to contain the mess she had unleashed, but nothing they did seemed to matter. The chaos spread too far, too fast. The authorities were overwhelmed, and Katya, from the safety of her apartment, could only watch the unfolding disaster with a sense of triumph.

She had orchestrated it all with meticulous precision—the poisonings, the false trails, the misdirection that had led them down countless dead ends. She had created an unstoppable force. She had turned death itself into a tool, an instrument of her ascension. Katya had always seen herself as something more than human—something divine, something meant to transcend the mortal plane. The souls of the dead, she believed, whispered their secrets to her, guided her, lifted her up. She had become the master of life and death, and the world, in all its weakness, had been laid bare before her in her five laws of power.

But now, as the days stretched on, the weight of her victory began to press down on her in ways she hadn't expected. Sitting alone in her apartment, surrounded by the flickering glow of her computer screens and the cold, sterile silence of the room, Katya felt something she hadn't felt in a long time. Doubt.

The walls, once familiar, now felt imprisoning. The voices that had once filled her with a sense of power now seemed distant, disjointed. They still whispered to her, yes —but the words, once comforting and guiding, had started to fade, losing their clarity. The whispers were no longer those of loyal followers or newly claimed souls, but a jumbled cacophony, a distorted chorus that tugged at her mind. Was it the weight of her actions finally catching up with her? Or was this the crack in her delusion, the first sign that everything she had built was beginning to crumble from the inside?

In her mind, Katya had envisioned her victory as a grand ascension—a moment where the world would kneel before her, acknowledging her as a new force of power, a new kind of deity. She had seen herself at the pinnacle, casting aside the frailty of human existence, ruling from a place where nothing could touch her, where the very fabric of life and death was at her command. But now, with the world still spiraling into an unpredictable storm of confusion, Katya was forced to confront a terrible question: What had she truly won?

The weight of her actions—the countless lives she had taken to fuel her vision—pressed on her heart. She had risen to power through death, through destruction, and now, in the stillness of her apartment, she could feel the consequences in her very bones. She had always believed that her purpose was justified, that the world needed to be purged in order to make way for something new. But what had she created? A world in ruins, a world filled with panic, broken people, and an unstable government. Was this truly the new world she had envisioned? Was this chaos really the future she had wanted to build? Or was it simply the aftermath of her own unchecked ambition?

As the silence deepened around her, the cracks in her delusion of divinity became harder to ignore. In her quest to transcend the human condition, she had become disconnected from the very world she sought to control. Her victory, she realized, had come at the cost of her own humanity. She had stripped away everything that made her human—the empathy, the compassion, the connections to the people around her—and in doing so, she had lost something she had never even realized she needed. Peace.

Katya had thought she could control it all, that she could take what was hers and mold the world into her vision. But now, as she sat in the silence, it seemed that the price she had paid—the countless lives she had stolen—was more than she had been willing to acknowledge.

The souls that she once felt guiding her now felt like a burden, like weights pressing down on her chest. They didn't feel like loyal followers; they felt like tormented ghosts. The silence of her apartment, once a place of refuge, now felt suffocating, as if the walls were closing in on her.

Katya's mind wandered, and for the first time, she wondered if everything had been a mistake. Had she truly ascended, or had she merely created a kingdom built on sand, a castle of blood and death that could never stand? She had believed she was a force of nature—unstoppable, untouchable. But the realization was dawning: perhaps the real power had never been in the control of life and death, but in knowing when to stop, in understanding that true ascension might not lie in domination, but in the ability to coexist with those who shared the world.

But it was too late for that now. The seeds of her actions had already been sown, and they were growing—in ways she couldn't fully comprehend. The world had changed, irrevocably. And Katya, once so certain of her purpose, was now left alone with the crushing weight of the empire she had created, wondering if she had truly won—or if she had just destroyed everything in her path.

In the silence, Katya realized the terrifying truth: Victory, in her case, was an illusion. The moment she had taken control of death, she had become bound to it. And in the end, it wasn't the world she had been shaping—it was herself that she had been losing all along.

9
THE FINAL TRUTH

Washington, D.C. - Early Summer 2020
Étienne sat in his small, sterile hotel room, the weight of his thoughts pressing down on him like an invisible force. The dim, flickering lamp cast long shadows against the walls, and the quiet hum of the city outside seemed distant and insignificant in comparison to the chaos that had unfolded in the last few months. He stared at his laptop, his fingers hovering over the keyboard as his mind raced through the tangled web of evidence he had gathered. Each new piece of information he uncovered seemed to only deepen the mystery, pulling him further into the storm of Katya's influence.

The investigation had consumed him. Every waking moment had been spent chasing her, trying to put together the pieces of a puzzle that was far larger and far darker than he had ever anticipated. What had begun as a simple case of murder had quickly turned into something far more sinister. Katya wasn't just a killer. She was something else entirely—a force. She wasn't operating alone; she was the leader of something bigger, something that had gained momentum far beyond her initial actions.

Her followers—her disciples—were spreading like a virus. What had once been whispers of admiration had grown into a full-fledged movement, fueled by her twisted vision of power and transcendence. Each new message from her followers revealed the depth of her reach, and with every communication, the scale of her influence seemed to expand. Katya had tapped into something primal —something that spoke to the darkest corners of the human soul. She promised control. She promised ascension. She promised power beyond the mortal realm, and people were believing it.

The authorities were still trying to catch up. The news was flooded with reports of the mysterious deaths, the chaos in the prison systems, the apparent breakdown of societal order. But none of it had been linked to Katya yet. The police, the FBI—they were all still chasing dead ends. Katya had outsmarted them all. She wasn't just hiding in the shadows anymore; she had become the shadow itself. And the more Étienne dug into her network, the more he realized that she had already won.

But then, as if sensing his relentless pursuit, she made her next move.

A new message popped up on his screen. He froze. It was a video.

Étienne's heart skipped a beat. Every fiber of his being screamed for him to ignore it—to stop right now and destroy the file. But he couldn't bring himself to look away. His fingers trembled as he clicked play.

The screen flickered to life, and there she was. Katya. Sitting perfectly still, her face composed, her eyes sharp and confident. She looked almost serene, her features unmarked by the chaos she had caused. She was a picture of control, calmness, and unnerving certainty. The camera zoomed in, capturing every minute detail of her face. Her lips curled into the smallest of smiles, a knowing, almost affectionate expression—as if she were addressing someone on a personal level, rather than the entire world.

"Étienne," she began, her voice coming through soft and honeyed, as though they were old friends. "I've been waiting for you. I knew you'd come. We're so close, aren't we? The world is in the palm of my hand, and there's nothing anyone can do to stop me."

Her words sent a shiver down Étienne's spine. She spoke with such conviction, as if she had already crossed the threshold into something greater than herself. There was no hesitation in her tone, no fear, just an overwhelming certainty in her words that unsettled him deeply. This wasn't the voice of a criminal trying to justify her actions—it was the voice of someone who genuinely believed she had ascended to a higher plane, that she was destined for this.

She leaned forward slightly, her eyes locking onto the screen as if she were staring directly at Étienne, piercing him with her gaze. "But you..." she continued, her voice turning almost tender, as if she were speaking to a long-lost friend. "You could join me, you know. You don't have to fight this. You don't have to chase shadows anymore. I have control. I can give you everything you've ever wanted. Together, we could shape the future. A future where we are untouchable."

Étienne's breath caught in his chest. He had always known that Katya was dangerous, but hearing her speak like this—so calmly, so assured of her own righteousness— made him realize just how far gone she truly was. She wasn't just some criminal mastermind anymore; she was sick with power, intoxicated by her own delusions of grandeur. She saw herself as a prophet, a messiah, leading the world into an era of total control, with herself at the helm.

His first instinct was to hit the power button, to erase the video and pretend he had never seen it. To destroy the evidence, to sever his last connection to her. But Étienne didn't do it. Instead, he sat frozen, staring at the screen. He couldn't look away. This video wasn't just a taunt—it was a message. A confession. She was inviting him to join her. She wanted him to see the truth, to come to her side. In a twisted way, this was Katya's attempt at reconciliation, at bringing him into her vision of the world.

As the video ended, a new window popped up on his screen. It was an encrypted file—a location. A time.

Étienne's heart pounded in his chest as the realization hit him. This wasn't a random message. It wasn't just a warning. It was a promise—something was going to happen, and it was happening tonight. Katya had planned this moment with the same cold precision that had guided every step of her rise to power.

The clock was ticking.

Étienne didn't hesitate. He grabbed his coat and rushed out of the room, the weight of his responsibility pressing down on him harder than ever before. He wasn't sure if he could stop her, but he couldn't let her control the narrative any longer. Katya's movement was growing—spreading like wildfire—and if he didn't act now, it might be too late to bring it all crashing down.

Tonight was the night. It was time to face Katya—once and for all.

· · ·

The Showdown

The streets of Washington, D.C. were eerily quiet that night, a heavy calm that contrasted sharply with the storm of thoughts swirling in Étienne's mind. His footsteps echoed through the otherwise empty corridors of the hotel, each sound feeling like a drumbeat marking the countdown to a confrontation he had spent months preparing for. The stakes had never been higher, and yet, in the pit of his stomach, he felt an unsettling sense of finality. If he didn't stop her tonight—if he didn't somehow find a way to end this nightmare—Katya would only continue to grow in power, building her twisted vision one follower at a time.

She was becoming more than a person, Étienne realized. She was becoming an idea, a movement. Her actions, her words, the very aura she projected were now infectious. People were flocking to her, abandoning everything they knew for the promise of power, immortality, and transcendence. In her mind, the world was collapsing, and she was simply the one chosen to usher in the new era.

But Étienne wasn't about to let her succeed. Not tonight.

The encrypted message had led him to this point: an abandoned building on the outskirts of the city. A structure that had once served as a hideout for activists—an ironic choice for Katya, considering how much she now sought to control. The building had been forgotten, like so many of the lives Katya had discarded in her path. Its broken windows, cracked walls, and creeping decay mirrored the ideology she sought to impose on the world—chaos, destruction, and ultimate control.

Étienne stepped cautiously, his senses heightened with each step. His fingers brushed against the handle of the gun hidden beneath his jacket. It was a precaution, not one he hoped to use, but he knew well enough that he couldn't trust her—or her followers. If things escalated, he would have to be ready.

The hallway stretched on in front of him, the shadows thick and oppressive. Every movement felt amplified in the silence that surrounded him. He couldn't afford to be careless now. Katya was elusive, always one step ahead, playing a game of psychological warfare from the moment they first crossed paths. Was she really deluded? He couldn't help but ask himself. Or had he underestimated her from the start? Was she truly capable of seeing her vision through, no matter the cost? Had she already won in her own mind?

The building felt like it was closing in on him, as if the very structure of the place was holding its breath, waiting for the inevitable confrontation. He crept forward, moving deeper into the abandoned space, his eyes darting around every corner, every shadow. Then, through a doorway, he saw it.

At the center of the room stood Katya.

She was a figure in the dim light, almost ethereal in her presence. Her hair cascaded around her shoulders like a dark halo, and the silence around her seemed to hum with an energy that was both unnerving and magnetic. The air itself felt charged. But what truly struck Étienne was her expression. It was tranquil, almost serene, yet there was something in her eyes—a look of certainty, of absolute belief in what she was about to accomplish.

And she wasn't alone.

Surrounding her were a dozen figures—her followers. They stood in a semi-circle around her, eyes wide with zealous devotion. Their faces were a mix of reverence and awe, their postures stiff with anticipation, as though they were awaiting a divine command. These weren't just ordinary people anymore. They were disciples, willing to lay down their lives for her vision, for whatever promise she had made them. They had become the first wave of a new movement, one that could reshape the world in Katya's image.

The scene before Étienne seemed like something out of a religious ritual, a cult-like gathering with Katya at the center, playing the part of a prophet, the people around her like eager acolytes. And Étienne couldn't help but wonder—had she truly believed that she could ascend to a place above humanity? Had she become what she had always wanted to be—a god, with the power to shape the future?

He stepped forward, his pulse quickening, the weight of the moment almost suffocating. His mind raced—this was it, the culmination of everything he had fought for.

And then, it happened.

"Étienne."

Her voice cut through the silence, soft, almost too soft for the situation. But there was power in it. Her tone was serene, but it held a certain weight, a confidence that sent a chill down his spine. Katya wasn't just speaking to him. She was acknowledging him as a part of her world now. He had found her, and she had known he would. In that moment, Étienne realized how far gone she truly was. She wasn't just toying with him anymore; she was enthralled by the idea that she was playing a part in something much larger than herself.

"You found me," Katya continued, her smile widening, her eyes glinting with a mix of amusement and sadness. There was a strange compassion in her gaze, as if she was the only one who truly understood the truth of the world. "I knew you would. You always chase the truth, don't you,

Étienne? But you don't see it, do you? You can't even comprehend the world that's coming."

Étienne's jaw tightened. He stepped closer, his voice steady but filled with a simmering anger. "This is it, Katya. This is where it ends. You've crossed every line. You've made a choice, and I'm here to stop you. It's over."

Katya's smile didn't falter. It only grew. Her followers remained still, their eyes fixed on her, as though they were waiting for her to speak the word that would make everything clear.

But Étienne wasn't afraid of her. He wasn't intimidated by the movement she had created or the false vision of power she held so tightly to. No, what terrified him was the realization that she truly believed in it—that this was what she had wanted all along. The chance to reshape the world. To make herself godlike in the eyes of those willing to listen.

But he couldn't let that happen.

This was the moment. The last stand. If he failed now, Katya would have the power to reshape everything, to tear apart the very fabric of society. He couldn't let that happen. Not when he still had a chance to stop her.

And so, with a steadying breath, Étienne squared his shoulders, ready to face whatever came next. This was it— the showdown between the man who clung to the last remnants of justice and the woman who believed she was the harbinger of a new world. And only one of them would walk away.

The Confrontation

The air between Étienne and Katya was thick with tension, electric with the weight of everything that had led them to this moment. Each breath felt like it could be the last. His fingers twitched toward the gun at his side, but he stopped himself. In his mind, he knew that force alone wouldn't end this. No bullet, no weapon could bring her down—not now. The problem wasn't physical power. It was something far more dangerous. Katya had already become a force—a movement, a vision—and the world had already begun to bend to her influence. Her followers, standing motionless around her, were like devotees, their eyes glazed over with reverence, as if she were more than just a woman. To them, she was divinity incarnate, and they were entranced, believing in her power and the promise she had made: that she could give them everything they had ever desired.

Katya wasn't just a killer anymore. She was a messiah in her own eyes, and that belief radiated from her in the way she stood, the way she spoke, and the way she carried herself. As Étienne stood at the threshold of her domain, the entire room seemed to pulse with her self-assurance, a force so strong it could almost be felt in the air.

She turned fully to face him, her eyes locking with his. There was no fear in her gaze—only something far colder, far more calculating. She was in control, and she knew it.

"I know what you're thinking, Étienne," she said, her voice low, almost gentle, but with an edge of something sharp, something terrifying. "You think I'm crazy. You think I've lost control. But I haven't. I'm the only one who has true control."

Her voice rose slightly, and there was a flicker in her eyes—a flash of intensity that showed just how deeply she believed in her delusions. For a moment, it was as if her mask was slipping, and the true force of her obsession with power began to show through.

"They will understand," she continued, her voice growing more urgent, more convincing, almost as if she were trying to sell her vision, not just explain it. "They will all understand. They already do. Death is just the beginning, Étienne. The dead speak to me. They guide me. They have for years."

Katya's breath quickened, and the fervor in her voice became palpable. She wasn't just speaking to him anymore. It was as though she were speaking to the world, broadcasting her truth—one that she had clung to for so long that it had become the only thing that mattered.

"And soon," she continued, eyes dark with promise, "I'll be able to speak to all of them. I'll command them. I'll reshape this world." Her voice, now filled with an eerie certainty, reverberated around the room, and Étienne felt the weight of her words press against him. She had crossed a line, and in her mind, there was no going back. Her reality had shifted to the point where she truly believed she could summon the dead and control their spirits—where her will could bend the world itself.

Étienne took a deliberate step forward, his gaze never leaving hers. His pulse was steady, his thoughts sharp. He couldn't let himself be swayed by the strange pull of her presence. He had to remain grounded, to remind himself that this woman—this thing in front of him—was no god, but a deluded murderer who had convinced herself of her own divinity.

"You've lost yourself, Katya," Étienne said quietly, his voice steady, yet filled with an edge of sorrow. "You've killed, manipulated, and hurt everyone you've touched in the name of a fantasy." His eyes bore into her, searching for any trace of the woman she used to be, any sign of humanity that might still be there. "What you're hearing...

are the echoes of your own guilt—and it's eating you alive."

Her eyes flickered, just for a brief moment, but it was enough. The brief flash of doubt—a crack in her facade— was all Étienne needed to see that she still felt it. The weight of everything she had done was getting to her, even if she wouldn't admit it. The souls of her victims, the lives she had stolen, were haunting her. They weren't whispering to her as guiding voices anymore; they were closing in, suffocating her, reminding her that the price of her power had been too high.

But just as quickly, that doubt was buried beneath layers of defiance. Katya took a sharp breath, her hands trembling slightly as she steadied herself. The look in her eyes hardened once again—the mask back in place. She was slipping deeper into her delusion, and Étienne knew she had already gone too far.

"You don't understand," she spat, her voice sharp now, with a dangerous edge. "You never did. You're just like them, Étienne. You're still chasing the illusion of control." Her gaze grew darker, more intense, and she stepped closer to him, as though closing the distance between them would somehow solidify her claim on reality. "But I—" She paused again, the words catching in her throat, a momentary hesitation before she let it go, her breath ragged with the intensity of her conviction. "I've ascended beyond that."

The finality in her words was chilling. She had crossed a threshold, and now, there was no turning back. To Katya, there was nothing left but her vision—her godhood, her power—and she couldn't allow anyone to take that from her. Not even Étienne, who had been chasing her through every twist and turn, trying to make sense of the madness she had created.

For Katya, the endgame was in sight. She didn't see herself as a villain anymore. She was a visionary. And in her mind, she had already won.

Étienne, however, stood firm. The weight of his responsibility was not lost on him. He had to stop her, not just for the world, but for her, as well. Because, deep down, he knew that the woman standing in front of him—this twisted version of the woman she had once been—would destroy herself in her pursuit of power. Her ascension was built on the foundation of lies, of blood, and of manipulation. There was no salvation in what she had become.

And with that understanding, Étienne took another step closer. This was the moment. The confrontation would determine everything. Would he be able to stop her before it was too late? Would he be able to break the delusion, shatter the fantasy she had built for herself?

In that moment, the entire world seemed to hang in the balance.

The Unraveling

The air in the room thickened as Katya's followers grew restless.

The tension in the room was palpable, a suffocating weight that pressed against Étienne's chest. The followers—her loyal disciples, her blind believers—shifted on their feet, their eyes fixed on Katya with a mix of awe and fear. They had been waiting for this moment, a moment they believed would bring about a new era. Their devotion had already consumed them, each one enraptured by Katya's words, her promises of transcendence, of power, of control over death itself. To them, this wasn't madness—it was a divine truth unfolding.

Étienne could feel the heaviness in the air, as though the very room itself was holding its breath, waiting for the inevitable. His thoughts raced. He had studied Katya, followed her every move, but this moment was something else entirely. She had crossed a line he couldn't have anticipated. The voices in her head—the ones that had driven her from a simple killer to a twisted prophet—had become her guiding force, her anchor to whatever world she thought she was living in. And now, those voices had drowned out everything else.

Katya no longer saw reality. She was lost in the delusion of her own creation. She truly believed she could transcend life and death—that she was more than human, a being above the laws of nature. Étienne, however, understood the truth better than anyone in that room. There was no power in death, no salvation in destruction. Just an abyss of darkness that threatened to swallow her whole.

"The dead will rise."

The words that left Katya's lips were soft, but they were shrouded in conviction, as though she were speaking a prophecy. It wasn't an announcement—it was a prayer. Her hands shot up toward the ceiling, as though she could summon the dead with a mere gesture.

Étienne felt the room tremble, as though the very building itself were reacting to her words. The air around him grew electric, charged with an ominous energy. He had seen the signs before—her delusions were getting worse, more elaborate, but this was the moment where it all came together. She truly believed it. And if he didn't act now, everything would spiral out of control.

The walls had been reinforced. Katya had prepared for this, and Étienne knew it. This wasn't some random, chaotic outburst. Katya had designed this entire space—a trap built with meticulous care. Every detail had been considered. The structure of the building, the layout of the room, the reinforcement of the walls—it was all meant to keep anyone out, or in, as needed. This was her sanctum, a place where she could perform whatever twisted ritual she believed would usher in her godhood.

But Étienne also knew the truth—none of it would work. She wasn't preparing to transcend reality. She was convinced she had already done so. In her mind, she had already ascended, risen above the world she once knew. The walls and the trap were just the symbols of her final delusion—a manifestation of her desire to control everything, even death.

And that made her dangerous.

Étienne's heart raced. The moment of reckoning was here. He didn't have much time. The followers, their eyes glazed with fanaticism, were already beginning to stir. Their devotion to Katya clouded their judgment, leaving them vulnerable to her influence. They would do anything she asked—anything she commanded. And if they thought she was on the brink of accomplishing something miraculous—something divine—they wouldn't hesitate to follow her into the abyss.

The room was beginning to feel claustrophobic, the walls pressing in as the air grew thick with anticipation. Étienne's every instinct screamed at him to act, to intervene before it was too late. But how could he stop her when her followers were this far gone?

He needed to snap her out of it. He needed to break through the haze of her delusions, to remind her of the woman she once was. If there was any chance left for her— any trace of the person she had been before she had descended into madness—it was now, in this fleeting moment before the world truly fractured.

"Listen to me, Katya," he said urgently, his voice cutting through the rising tension. He took a step closer, his gaze locked on hers. "You don't have to do this. You can still stop this." He felt his words hang in the air, desperate but steady. "You're not a god—you're just a woman who's lost her way."

For a moment, there was a flicker of recognition in her eyes—an almost imperceptible pause, as if something inside her stirred. The cold, unwavering certainty in her gaze softened, just a little. He had gotten through, even if only for a second.

But then, like a switch flipping, the delusion flared back to life, stronger than ever, more impenetrable than before. Her eyes hardened, the softness gone, replaced by the same manic, godlike certainty she had clung to for so long.

"No," she said firmly, her voice cutting through the tension. "I am a god."

The words hung in the air like a verdict—final, unyielding. There was no room for doubt in her voice, no room for compromise. The moment had passed. Katya had fully embraced the delusion. In her mind, she had already transcended—and nothing, not even Étienne, could bring her back.

And then everything erupted.

In a split second, the atmosphere shifted. The followers, who had been standing still, as if waiting for divine instruction, suddenly sprang into action. Some cried out in unison, others knelt in worship, but all of them were lost in their belief. The energy in the room shifted, turning chaotic. Étienne's mind raced as the dangerous realization hit him

—it was happening. Katya had convinced them all that she was their salvation. She was their goddess.

The room felt as though it were coming apart at the seams. Katya's delusions had become a self-fulfilling prophecy. Her belief in her own ascension was now feeding her power. The trap she had built was working—and the world outside this room was slipping further away.

Étienne's fingers tightened around his gun. He didn't know what was about to happen, but he had no choice. He had to act. He had to stop her—before she could drag everyone down with her.

10

THE COLLAPSE

Washington, D.C. - Midnight

The building trembled, as though the very walls themselves were beginning to crack under the weight of Katya's delusions. Étienne stumbled, disoriented, but quickly regained his footing. His eyes searched the darkness, the flickering lights casting long, distorted shadows on the walls. The air felt charged, as if something supernatural was unfolding before him. The hum of machinery reverberated in his bones, and distant voices—soft, unrecognizable—filtered through the oppressive silence. The followers were no longer human; they were shadows of themselves, their minds consumed, hollow-eyed and lost in her twisted vision of power.

Katya stood in the center of it all, her hands raised high, as though she were summoning something far beyond the earthly realm. Her fingers twisted and curled, an unnatural conductor orchestrating an invisible force. Her lips moved, but the words never reached his ears. Instead, there was an erratic, primal energy that seemed to vibrate through the air, like a pulse that threatened to swallow the room whole.

"Katya!" Étienne's voice broke through the tension. His shout was raw, desperate, a last attempt to reach her through the fog of madness. "Stop this! You're not a god, you're just a woman hiding from your guilt. You're destroying everything you ever wanted."

For a moment, Katya's eyes snapped open, the intensity in them sharp, unwavering. The room seemed to hold its breath. Her followers stood motionless, as if frozen in time, each one a silent soldier in her war for control. They were waiting for her command, waiting for her to decide who would live and who would die.

Guilt. It was a word that cut through the air, sharp and accusing. Katya repeated it, as though testing its weight in her mind. "Guilt?" Her voice was soft, detached. There was no anger in it, only a cold finality, as if the very concept of guilt had become irrelevant to her. "You still don't understand, Étienne. You think you know me, but you don't. Guilt has no place in my world anymore. I am beyond it."

The words hung in the air, thick and suffocating, as she stepped closer to him. Her eyes never left his, as if locking him into a gaze that was meant to pierce through the layers of his soul. The tension between them was palpable, electric.

"I'm not hiding anymore," she said, her voice growing stronger. "I've accepted who I really am. And now... I'll make everyone see. See what I've seen. Feel what I've felt. I will be the one to choose who lives and who dies."

Étienne's heart hammered in his chest, his breath shallow, but he couldn't afford to falter. He was running out of time. Every instinct told him that this was a moment of reckoning—not just for her, but for the world she was on the verge of destroying. But he knew—he knew that the only way to stop her was to pierce through the madness. There had to be something, a crack in her delusion, a moment of humanity left beneath the surface. He couldn't give up. Not now.

"Katya," he said, his voice lower, quieter now, almost like a whisper between two old friends, "Do you remember your brother? Donovan? You said you killed him to take control of his soul. But you've never had control. You've only been running from the truth. Your brother's death isn't what made you powerful. It's what made you broken."

Her eyes flashed, and for the briefest of moments, the cold, calculating mask slipped. There was a flicker of vulnerability in her gaze, something human. Something familiar. The moment was so fleeting, so fragile, that Étienne almost couldn't believe it. But just as quickly as it had come, it vanished. The walls inside her mind slammed back into place, sealing away any trace of the woman she once was.

"No," she said, her voice quieter now, almost desperate, as though clinging to a fragile thread of justification. "You don't understand. Donovan's death gave me everything. It was the only way to understand the world. I had to make him pay. And now... now I will take what's mine. I will reshape everything."

The room filled with an eerie chant. Her followers, synchronized in their trance, began to speak in unison, their voices like a chant from some ancient, forbidden ritual: "Death is power. Death is ascension." Their eyes were wild, their faces empty, as if they had already surrendered themselves to her vision of the world.

Étienne's heart sank as the realization hit him like a punch to the gut. This wasn't just about her anymore—it was about an entire movement. Katya had become the center of a belief system that was far more dangerous than he had ever imagined. Words, logic, reason—none of it mattered anymore. Her delusions were so ingrained in her mind, so far-reaching, that even the truth of her actions couldn't break through.

And yet, Étienne couldn't stop. He couldn't give up. If words couldn't reach her, if logic had failed, then there was only one thing left.

The Final Gamble

The moment stretched thin, suspended in the thickening air. Étienne's fingers brushed against the inside of his coat pocket, feeling the cool, smooth glass of the vial nestled there. He had carried it with him for weeks now, always hoping he wouldn't need it—hoping that somehow, he could find another way to stop Katya. The vial was small, its contents a clear liquid, and it felt like a weight in his pocket, a constant reminder of just how desperate the situation had become.

The vial contained a counteragent, a specially formulated substance designed to neutralize the toxins Katya had introduced into the U.S. prison system. The poison she had carefully distributed in secret had wreaked havoc, and if Étienne could inject the antidote directly into her bloodstream, it would block the poison's effects, rendering her lethal scheme ineffective. The implications were monumental. This single action could undo months of chaos.

But there was a catch. Using it on Katya wouldn't just stop the poison—it would disorient her, possibly cloud her mind, break the connection she had with her followers. And it could even have unpredictable consequences, causing a momentary lapse in her power, a temporary fracture in the delusion that she had woven so carefully. It was a gamble, and Étienne knew it was his last chance. If this didn't work, nothing would. And if it did, who knew what kind of havoc it would unleash on her already fragile psyche?

He took a steadying breath, his fingers curling around the vial. His heartbeat quickened. The weight of the decision pressed down on him—was he really willing to risk everything for a chance to stop her? Could he live with the consequences of what he might have to do? There was no turning back. He had carried this vial for one reason: to stop her, even if it meant breaking her mind further, even if it meant destroying the last remnants of the woman she had once been.

But as his hand reached into his coat pocket, everything around him seemed to change.

The sensation in his stomach intensified, like something foreign was twisting inside him, pulling at his insides. It wasn't just the poison in the air—it was something deeper, something more insidious. The atmosphere itself felt thick, suffocating. The very air felt charged, as though the room had become a pressure cooker, ready to explode. The hum of the machinery in the background grew louder, more oppressive, reverberating like the sound of a thousand insects buzzing in his ears.

Katya's voice rose again, but this time, it was different. There was a distortion in it, a rising pitch that made her words sound alien, unrecognizable. It was as if her voice had become something otherworldly, like it was being warped by an unseen force.

"You think you can stop me?" she sneered, her voice

rising higher and higher, the tone becoming almost shrill. It was as if her very being was beginning to unravel. "You can't stop what's already started, Étienne. You are nothing but a footnote in my story. I've already crossed the line. There's no going back."

Her eyes locked with his again—piercing, frenzied, filled with an insanity that sent a shiver down his spine. There was no vulnerability there now. No trace of the woman he had once known. Just madness, pure and raw. The smile that twisted her lips was savage, almost animalistic. It was the smile of someone who had gone beyond the point of no return, someone who had already abandoned the last vestiges of humanity.

Étienne could feel his chest tightening. Every instinct in his body screamed at him to act—to make a move, to stop her before it was too late. But the world around him seemed to distort. The air itself was warping, thickening, as though the room was shrinking, pressing in on him from all sides. His breathing became shallow, and his mind raced, trying to make sense of the surreal, suffocating atmosphere.

And then, with a sudden, deafening crash, the ceiling above them cracked. A deep rumble shook the entire building, and the sound of splitting concrete filled the air. It felt like the earth itself was tearing apart. Debris rained down from above, and Étienne barely had time to duck as jagged pieces of rubble cascaded through the room, narrowly missing him.

Chaos erupted.

Katya's followers screamed, their once-still forms scrambling in every direction, their minds no longer tethered to the woman they had worshipped. Panic rippled through the room as they tried to shield themselves from the falling rubble. Their devotion to her had cracked, just like the ceiling above them. But it wasn't enough to break the hold she had on them entirely. They moved in disjointed movements, their eyes still glazed over, their bodies responding to her commands like puppets on strings.

Étienne's heart pounded harder, and in that moment, everything seemed to slow down. His eyes scanned the room, searching for any advantage, any opportunity to act. The air was thick with dust and the echoes of Katya's deranged chanting, but amidst the chaos, a fleeting moment of clarity cut through. This was his chance.

In the confusion, Katya's attention faltered, her gaze momentarily distracted by the falling debris. Her followers, though still entranced, were thrown off balance by the destruction around them. This was the opening Étienne needed. He couldn't hesitate anymore.

He pulled the vial from his coat pocket, his hands steady despite the adrenaline pumping through his veins. He moved quickly, every step calculated, his mind laser-focused. He had no time to second-guess himself. There was no more room for hesitation. With a swift motion, he unscrewed the vial and prepared the syringe.

But just as his fingers closed around the needle, Katya's voice broke through the chaos again, cutting through the air like a blade.

"No," she whispered, her tone thick with an eerie finality. "You can't stop me, Étienne. You will never stop me."

Her voice rose to a fever pitch, distorted and shrill, but as Étienne lunged forward to close the distance, time seemed to twist once again. The room shook violently, and the shadows around him grew darker, more oppressive. It was as if the very fabric of reality was warping, pulling him into an abyss where nothing made sense anymore.

Everything was on the line now.

The Collapse of Control

The room was a chaotic battleground of shattered walls and broken lives. Debris scattered across the floor, dust clinging to the air, and the harsh flicker of emergency lights was like the final breaths of a dying world. Katya's followers had turned from zealous devotion to panic; fear had replaced their blind faith. Some stumbled over one another, lost in confusion, others desperately trying to return to their trance-like state, as if the foundation of their belief could still be salvaged. But that foundation was cracked, the moment of disruption too much for them to ignore. Étienne saw his opening.

His pulse hammered in his ears as he moved, weaving between bodies in disarray. His steps were deliberate but swift. The vial of antidote in his hand felt heavy with significance. This was it—the final move. There was no turning back now. If he hesitated even for a moment, it could all end in catastrophe. His mind raced, replaying every painful decision, every painful encounter leading up to this point. He couldn't afford to think about failure. He couldn't afford to dwell on the past. This was his last chance.

The weight of his decision hit him in waves. He wasn't just fighting to stop Katya—he was fighting to stop the collapse of everything she represented. Every life she had destroyed, every soul she had twisted, now came down to this singular moment. He had to stop her. He had to.

But before he could get close enough, Katya's head snapped in his direction. Her face was twisted with fury, but it was more than that—there was a deep satisfaction there, too, as if she were savoring the moment before she struck. She was no longer just the woman he had known; she was something far darker, something beyond reason. Her delusions had transformed her into a force that Étienne could barely comprehend.

"You can't stop me!" she screamed. Her voice was shrill and violent, vibrating through the tension in the room. It was a primal shout, as if every ounce of control had been ripped from her and replaced with blind, unrelenting rage. Her arms flung out, reaching for something sharp from the wreckage of the ceiling. She had found a jagged piece of metal, a weapon now in her hands, and she gripped it like a lifeline.

Étienne's body tensed, his heart thundering as he sprinted forward. He had no other choice. The antidote was now his only weapon—his only hope. But before he could get close enough, Katya's wild eyes locked onto his, and the chaos in the room seemed to fade into the background. In that brief, unbearable moment, there was nothing but her and him. And the destructive force she had become.

"Stop!" Étienne shouted, but his voice was swallowed by the cacophony of madness around them. He couldn't break through to her. Not with words. Not anymore.

Katya's face twisted into something unrecognizable—a mixture of ecstasy and rage, an expression far beyond human. "I am beyond you," she hissed, and her laughter filled the space between them, haunting and unhinged.

With a surge of strength, she lunged at him, her sharp weapon slicing through the air. The blow came so quickly, it was almost too fast for Étienne to react. But in the split second before impact, he made his move.

He jabbed the syringe into her neck. The needle punctured her skin with a sickening pop, and for an instant, everything froze. The chaos around them, the cries of her followers, the sounds of crumbling debris—all fell silent.

For a single heartbeat, Katya stood still, her eyes wide with disbelief. Her breath was shallow, her body rigid, as if she couldn't understand what had just happened. She looked at the syringe in her neck, and her lips trembled as if she were trying to process the weight of the moment. Her expression shifted, a flicker of vulnerability in her eyes. But just for a second.

Then, the room was filled with the haunting sound of her low, guttural laugh. It started quietly, almost as if it were an afterthought, but then it grew, deep and distorted, reverberating through the space like the roar of some ancient force. It was an unholy sound—dark, almost primal —one that sent a chill down Étienne's spine. There was no relief. No moment of triumph. No crack in her delusion.

A twisted smile curved her lips as she whispered, "You think this is the end?"

The air around them seemed to thicken, the tension palpable. Her eyes, now wide and gleaming with an unsettling certainty, met his. "You can't stop what's already started, Étienne," she said, her voice now laced with venom. "I've crossed the line. There's no going back. I am beyond your reach."

Étienne's breath caught in his throat, the reality of the situation crashing over him in waves. The antidote hadn't worked. It hadn't shaken her. It hadn't broken the spell she'd cast over herself and her followers. This wasn't about logic anymore. This was about something far more dangerous—a belief so powerful, so unshakable, that it could bend the world to its will. She wasn't just delusional. She had created a new reality, and everyone in the room was either a part of it or in its way.

The ground beneath them seemed to tremble, the air vibrating with the intensity of her belief. The followers, still in their dazed stupor, began to murmur again, their voices rising in unison, chanting: "Death is power. Death is ascension."

But Étienne wasn't listening to them. He was listening to the sound of Katya's laugh, the sickening joy in it, the finality of her words. He had tried to reach her, tried to stop her, but there was no reasoning with someone who had become this untouchable, this consumed by her own delusions. He had failed.

But he couldn't stop fighting.

Through the dizziness of the moment, the overwhelming sense of hopelessness that threatened to swallow him, Étienne understood one crucial truth: the fight wasn't over. She had crossed a line, yes. But that didn't mean it was too late. There was always a way to stop madness—there had to be.

With a final surge of adrenaline, Étienne stepped closer, not to defeat her with violence, but to confront her—one last time.

The Beginning of the End

The chants of Katya's followers grew more disjointed by the second, their once-unified voices now a jumbled cacophony, like broken echoes ricocheting off the cracked walls of the room. Their once-zealous devotion, so carefully cultivated by Katya, was unraveling before Étienne's eyes. The shift in the atmosphere was palpable—what had once been a symbol of power, a unified movement, was now crumbling like a house of cards, one gust away from complete destruction.

Étienne stood frozen, his eyes locked on Katya, watching the woman he had chased, battled, and tried to understand, begin to fracture before him. Her expression shifted from defiance to confusion, her face contorting in a mix of disbelief and rage as she felt the effects of the counteragent seeping into her system. It was subtle at first, a slight weakening in her posture, a tremor in her voice—but then, like a dam breaking, it spread through her, consuming her every thought.

"You think this will stop me?" she spat, her voice low, but laced with venom. Her words, once powerful and clear, now felt disconnected, fragmented, like a broken record skipping in a room filled with noise. "You don't understand what I've become."

Even as she spoke, Étienne could hear the vulnerability that was slipping through her facade. Her voice wavered at the end, as if unsure of herself, as if the certainty that had once driven her every action was now faltering. The walls around her delusions, so carefully constructed over the years, were beginning to crack. But despite her weakening state, there was still a fire in her eyes, a raw intensity that made her dangerous in her desperation.

Her hands trembled slightly as they fell to her sides, and her gaze turned inward for a split second, as though she were trying to make sense of what was happening to her body. Étienne could see it in her eyes—the deepening confusion, the unraveling of her mind. The poison she had so meticulously injected into herself—the very thing that had kept her in control, that had given her the illusion of godhood—was now working against her. The counteragent he had injected was not a cure; it was a force of dissonance, fighting against the poison and creating a war inside her body, inside her very mind.

The atmosphere in the room grew heavier. The walls seemed to close in around them, and Étienne could feel the weight of her madness pressing in on him. The followers were still chanting, but their voices now lacked the certainty, the passion they once had. They were like drones, repeating words they no longer understood, no longer connecting to the vision they had once followed so blindly. The power Katya had wielded over them, that magnetic pull that had kept them enthralled, was slipping through her fingers, just as it was slipping through her own grip on reality.

Étienne didn't speak. He couldn't find the words that would break through her delusion anymore. This wasn't about logic or confrontation anymore. This was a battle between her mind and her body, between what she believed to be true and the reality that was slowly suffocating her.

He watched her—the woman who had once believed herself untouchable—now trembling, her face twitching as if battling an invisible war within her own flesh. She took a faltering step back, as if the ground beneath her were giving way. The madness, once so precise and controlled, now seemed raw and disordered, a force devouring itself. She was unraveling, but beneath it all, there remained a thread of defiance, a fierce will to prove she could endure this, that she could rise above this fragile moment.

Her followers, now lost and uncertain, turned to her for direction—but there was nothing left to lead them. Doubt flickered in their eyes as the truth of what had just unfolded began to settle in. They weren't witnessing the rise they had been promised. They were witnessing the gradual unraveling of their leader.

Étienne's heart pounded, but his thoughts were

strangely clear. The room felt like it was spinning, but the moment wasn't slipping away. The endgame had begun, and this was only the beginning. Katya's mind was fracturing, her grip on reality slipping, and yet there was still the faintest glimmer of her old confidence—the part of her that refused to acknowledge defeat.

He could see it in her eyes now. The terror. The disbelief. But even deeper than that, there was the acknowledgment that she had crossed a line from which there would be no return. She had embraced the darkness, and now the darkness was consuming her.

Her body lurched again, her hands grabbing her head, as though trying to hold her mind together. She staggered, then fell to her knees, her breath coming in ragged gasps. The counteragent was working, but it wasn't enough. The poison had spread too far. The delusion was too deeply ingrained.

"Stop..." Katya whispered, more to herself than to anyone else. She looked around, as if searching for something, anything that would restore the power she had once felt. But all that was left was the cold truth that she had lost control.

Étienne could only watch as she crumpled on the floor, a shattered version of the woman who had once believed herself to be a god. The followers—those few who hadn't yet fled—looked on in horror, unsure whether to continue their chants or run, unsure what to believe now that their leader was nothing more than a broken, desperate shell of the power they had once worshipped.

The world around them seemed to freeze in that moment, as if everything had come to a sudden, dramatic halt. The silence in the room was deafening, as Étienne stood there, watching her destruction, knowing that this was the beginning of the end—not just for Katya, but for everything she had tried to build. She had built an empire on madness and destruction, but it was now crumbling at her feet, piece by piece.

But even as she collapsed, Étienne knew that the hardest part was still to come. This was only the beginning.

11

SHATTERED REALITY

Washington, D.C. - The Final Confrontation
The world had unraveled.

Étienne stood at the heart of the devastation, surrounded by the chaos Katya had once controlled, now reduced to disarray. Her followers, those who had been so unwavering in their devotion to her twisted vision, had scattered in fear. Some fled into the collapsing ruins of the building, while others stood frozen, staring at Katya in shock. They were no longer the zealous, undying disciples they had once been. Now, they were just broken echoes of the people they used to be, their belief shattered, their purpose lost. The spell Katya had cast over them had broken, and the reality she had so carefully constructed was now crumbling like a house of cards.

For the first time in years, Katya was no longer the one with control.

Étienne watched her, his gaze unwavering. He could see the effect the counteragent had on her—her once-steady figure now swayed, the firmness she had always carried faltering. Her face, which had always been a mask of confidence and power, was now pale, her eyes wide and confused. There was no trace of the godlike certainty she had once wielded so easily. Beneath the madness, Étienne saw something more human, something more vulnerable: fear.

Fear had always been the true driving force behind Katya's actions, Étienne realized. Not power, not immortality—not godhood—but fear. Fear of loss. Fear of weakness. Fear of being nothing. She had spent years building an empire of manipulation and control, but she had never truly been in control. She had been terrified of what she might become if she let go, terrified of confronting the truth that she was, at her core, just like everyone else: fragile, fallible, human.

Katya's breath was ragged, and her hands shook as she looked at Étienne, her pride and defiance still trying to hold their ground. She took a step toward him, her voice hoarse and dripping with venom. "You think you can stop me?" she rasped, her words slurring slightly as the poison and counteragent warred inside her body. "You think the world will go back to normal? You don't understand, Étienne. You're too late. I've already won."

Étienne shook his head, not in disbelief but in sadness. The sadness of seeing someone he once tried to save, now so far gone, lost in a fantasy that could never be real. "You didn't win, Katya," he said quietly, his voice heavy with exhaustion, but steady with conviction. "You never understood what it meant to truly control anyone. You only saw the bodies. You never saw the people you left behind, the lives you destroyed. You weren't in control—you were terrified."

Katya's lips twisted into a bitter, almost sadistic smile. The corner of her mouth lifted in a grimace, a final defense against the growing fissures in her psyche. She reached down to the rubble at her feet, grabbing a shard of broken glass. The jagged edge caught the dim light of the room, reflecting her fractured mind. Her legs wobbled beneath her, but the shard was now a symbol of her last act of defiance, a weapon against the truth she couldn't face.

"You think I'm scared of you?" she spat, her voice cracking, the tremor in her words betraying the venom she tried to mask. She raised the shard of glass, brandishing it like a sword. "You don't get it. You're just a witness to the end of the world."

Étienne took a cautious step forward, but he kept his distance. He could see the desperation in her eyes. This wasn't about stopping her physically anymore. It wasn't about defeating her in the way he'd originally planned. This was about breaking the delusion that had kept her going for so long. The walls around her mind had started to crumble, and he had to make sure she faced what was left.

"Katya," he said, his voice now calm but heavy with empathy. "You've been running for so long. But there's no escape from the truth—not even in the afterlife you've imagined. What you've done doesn't make you a god. It makes you a monster."

The words hit her like a physical blow. She recoiled, and for just a brief, fleeting moment, Étienne saw the faintest crack of vulnerability in her eyes. But it was quickly swallowed up by the storm inside her mind. She gripped the shard of glass tighter, her fingers white as bone. Her breath quickened, shallow and frantic.

"You're wrong," she hissed, but her words faltered, the conviction slipping from her voice like sand through her fingers. It was clear now, more than ever, that she wasn't sure who she was trying to convince—Étienne or herself. "I am more powerful than anyone can understand. I'm invincible."

Étienne stepped closer, but his gaze never wavered. "Invincible?" he said, his tone softening. "Is that why you're scared right now? Because deep down, you know that you're just like everyone else. Vulnerable. Human."

Katya's face contorted in anguish. The look in her eyes was that of a person unraveling, clinging to the only thing that had kept her going for so long: her delusion of invincibility. Her fingers cracked as she tightened her grip on the glass, the shards cutting into her skin as she desperately clung to the last remnants of her power.

"No," she whispered, almost pleading with herself. "No, no, no! I am beyond this. I'm not just a woman. I'm a force."

Étienne's heart clenched, torn between the sadness he felt for her and the terrible knowledge that she was beyond saving. This was it. The truth was breaking through, but at what cost? She was still so lost in her madness that she couldn't see the truth for what it was.

"Katya, listen to me," he said softly, his voice almost a whisper now, filled with an undeniable tenderness. "You're not a god. You never were. But it's not too late. You can still stop this. You can still walk away."

But the madness that had taken root in her mind had reached its final crescendo. She wasn't listening anymore. The delusions were all she had left. The words he spoke were like whispers in the storm, lost in the chaos of her fractured psyche. She took one last, desperate step forward, raising the shard of glass high, her eyes burning with the last vestiges of her belief in her own power.

"I'll make you see," she screamed, her voice raw with desperation. "I'll make you feel the power I have—just like all of them!"

In that moment, Étienne knew this was it. This was her final attempt to exert control, to make the world see her as she had always seen herself: invincible. But the truth was clear now—Katya's world had crumbled. And no matter how much she tried to claw her way back, the end was inevitable. The only question was whether or not she would accept it.

The Final Choice

Time seemed to stretch, an unbearable tension filling the space between them. Étienne's mind raced, his thoughts spinning in a whirlwind of confusion, desperation, and clarity all at once. What could he do? How could he possibly stop her now? The room was falling apart around them, the air thick with the remnants of madness and chaos. Katya, a woman he had once known, now stood before him—a fractured version of the person she used to be, clinging desperately to the belief that she was something more than human, something untouchable.

She had always believed that power came from control, that immortality was born from domination. She had twisted herself into this shape, manipulated her followers, and convinced herself that she could transcend mortality. But Étienne knew better. He knew that it wasn't about stopping her actions anymore. The actions, the violence, the chaos—they were symptoms of a far deeper disease. It wasn't just the people she had hurt; it wasn't just the lives she had destroyed. It was her belief system that had to be shattered. She needed to see the truth, to understand that the strength she sought was never found in power or control. It was found in vulnerability. In humanity.

The clock was ticking. This was the moment.

Katya's eyes were wild, her breath quick and shallow, her entire body trembling with rage and disbelief. The shard of glass was still raised, her arm unsteady but determined. She was holding on to her delusions with everything she had left, and the weight of those delusions—the suffocating burden of the lies she had told herself for so long—was finally taking its toll. She could feel it. She could feel the shift, the instability in her own mind. But the glass in her hand felt like the last thread of control, the last piece of herself she hadn't yet lost.

Étienne could see it, the way she was fighting against the collapse of her own identity. And he knew, deep down, that this moment, this final choice, would decide everything.

His heart pounded in his chest as he took a deep breath, his hands steady despite the chaos. He couldn't afford to hesitate. He couldn't afford to give in to fear. With one fluid motion, he closed the distance between them, grabbing her wrist and twisting it just enough to disarm her. The glass shard fell to the ground with a shattering noise, echoing through the room like the final death knell of her delusions.

Katya gasped in pain, her body jerking with the unexpected force of the movement. But Étienne didn't let go. His grip tightened around her wrist, not with anger or violence, but with the kind of unyielding resolve that could only come from knowing what was at stake. His face was inches from hers, their breaths mingling in the charged silence that followed.

For a long, agonizing moment, neither of them moved. The world seemed to stop, and the only thing that remained was the unbearable tension between them. The glass lay shattered on the floor, a symbol of everything she had believed in, now meaningless.

And then, in the stillness, Étienne spoke. His voice was calm, but the words cut through the madness like a knife.

"Katya," he said softly, his tone steady, yet filled with a raw, almost sorrowful clarity. "Let it go. You're not a goddess. You're just a woman who's been hurt. And it's okay to be hurt. But it's not okay to hurt others because of it."

The words hit her like a physical blow. Her entire body tensed, as if the weight of his truth had finally cracked the armor she had built around herself. Her eyes flickered, a brief flash of something—humanity, vulnerability, fear— passing through them. For the first time in years, the mask of invincibility, the shield of godhood she had so desperately clung to, began to crumble.

Katya's face crumpled, the rage and defiance dissolving into something deeper. Something more painful. Her breath hitched, and for the first time in a long time, she seemed small. Broken. Human.

Étienne's heart ached at the sight. He could see it now, the vulnerability she had buried so deep inside herself. The hurt, the grief, the shame. All of it flooding to the surface. The woman who had once believed she could transcend the pain of this world, who had tried to destroy everything in order to rebuild it in her own image, was now standing before him, vulnerable and undone.

Her chest heaved with the weight of his words, and she stumbled backward slightly, as though the force of what she had tried to ignore for so long was finally too much to bear. The shard of glass, which had once felt like the ultimate symbol of her power, now lay useless on the ground. It was just a weapon. Just a tool she had used to defend herself from facing her own brokenness. And in that moment, it meant nothing.

Étienne released her wrist, but didn't step back. He stayed close, his eyes soft but unwavering. There was no anger left in him, only sorrow. For her. For what she had become. For the pain she had caused, and for the life she could have had—if only she had let herself be human.

"Katya," he said, his voice barely above a whisper. "You're not alone. It's not too late to stop running. You can still heal. But you have to let go. You have to face what you've done. Only then will you find the peace you've been searching for."

Her eyes filled with tears, her body trembling as if the weight of everything she had ever done was finally crashing down on her all at once. Her hands, still shaking, dropped to her sides. She was no longer holding onto the illusion of power. She was no longer holding onto the belief that she could control everything around her. For the first time in years, she was just a woman, standing in the ruins of her own creation.

For a long moment, neither of them moved. The room was silent except for the soft sound of her breathing.

And then, slowly, Katya collapsed to her knees. She wasn't crying. Not yet. But the tears were there, hovering just beneath the surface. The dam that had held back her emotions for so long was starting to crack. And in that moment, Étienne knew that the battle wasn't over. Not yet. But this was the beginning of something new.

The beginning of the end of her madness. The beginning of the end of her reign of terror.

But more than that, it was the beginning of the end of her isolation. She had spent so long trying to become a god, trying to rise above everything and everyone. But the truth was that she had only become more alone. And now, in her brokenness, Étienne was offering her a choice—a choice to stop running, to let go of the illusion of control, and to heal.

This moment, this final choice, was the most important one of her life.

And, in a way, it was the final choice of Étienne's too: to keep fighting for her, to keep reaching out, even when all seemed lost.

The End of the Delusion

The room stood in stillness, an eerie quiet settling over the wreckage like a suffocating blanket. It was as if time itself had slowed, holding its breath, waiting for what would come next. The chaos, the violence, the madness that had filled the air moments before now felt like a distant memory—replaced by the profound stillness that followed. The walls, cracked and scarred from the destruction Katya had wrought, now seemed to close in on the broken figure that was once the source of all that turmoil.

Katya collapsed to her knees, her body crumpling as the last vestiges of her delusion faded away. The delusion that had sustained her, that had convinced her she was above all others, that had driven her to manipulate, to kill, to destroy —was gone. Like a taut wire that had finally snapped under the pressure, the last threads of her twisted vision unraveled before Étienne's eyes.

Her breath came in ragged sobs, each gasp a release of years' worth of suppressed guilt, fear, and rage. She was no longer the woman who had orchestrated such destruction with a cold, calculating smile. She was no longer the power-hungry figure who had believed she could rise above it all. Now, she was just a woman—a broken, fragile woman—grieving the wreckage she had left behind.

"I'm sorry," she whispered, her voice cracked and broken, as though the words were too much for her to bear.

It was a small thing, an almost imperceptible admission. But for Étienne, it was everything. In those two words, Katya had finally confronted the truth she had spent so long avoiding. She had finally broken the illusion that had kept her trapped in a cycle of violence and self-delusion. And with that one quiet apology, the last shred of control she had over her fate slipped away.

Étienne could feel the weight of the moment in his chest, the burden of everything that had led up to this point. His hand, which had been gripping her wrist moments before, relaxed. He stepped back slowly, his gaze never leaving her.

There was a strange emptiness in the air now, an absence where once there had been so much rage and power. Katya, the woman who had bent the world to her will, the woman who had tried to make herself a god, was now reduced to a mere shell of herself. The look in her eyes was one of profound sorrow, but it was also the first glimpse of something else: vulnerability. Her reign, her empire of manipulation, had crumbled before the weight of the truth she had been running from.

For Étienne, there was no joy in seeing her brought low. No satisfaction in watching her fall from the pedestal she had constructed for herself. What he had hoped for, what he had prayed for all along, was that she would see herself for who she truly was. Not a goddess. Not an immortal force. Just a person—hurt, broken, and lost. And in that moment, she was facing that reality for the first time.

But it wasn't over yet.

Étienne's eyes moved from her to the devastation around them. The room, once a place of power, was now a graveyard of broken dreams and shattered lives. The remnants of her delusion, the pieces of the empire she had so carefully constructed, lay in ruins. Her followers—those who had once believed in her, who had bent their will to hers—were scattered, their minds fractured by the collapse of the illusion they had been living under. Some were still kneeling in stunned silence, unable to process what had just happened. Others were running, fleeing into the wreckage of the building like ants whose queen had just been destroyed.

Étienne's heart ached, not just for Katya, but for the countless people whose lives had been upended by her twisted vision. The damage she had done was too vast to comprehend in a single moment, and now the work to undo it was only just beginning. The world she had torn apart would need to be rebuilt. The minds she had manipulated, the lives she had destroyed—they would need to be healed, somehow.

But for now, for this moment, there was one undeniable truth: Katya's reign was over. The power she had held over so many had been broken, the delusion she had lived under shattered.

Étienne watched as she sat on the cold floor, her body still shaking with sobs, her hands clutching at the floor as though trying to hold herself together. He could see the regret in her eyes, the devastation that had overtaken her, but he didn't move to comfort her. This moment wasn't about redemption—it was about reality. She had made her choices. She had taken lives, destroyed futures, and manipulated people to the brink of insanity. There was no going back from that.

But perhaps, just perhaps, she could rebuild. Perhaps

she could heal. Perhaps the damage she had done didn't have to define her.

Étienne turned away from her, his heart heavy with the weight of all that had happened. The wreckage of the building was still unfolding, the reality of everything Katya had caused settling in. The path forward was unclear, the work ahead daunting, but the one thing Étienne knew for certain was that the war for her soul was over.

And now, it was time to rebuild.

This wasn't the end, not yet. But it was the end of the delusion that had driven Katya, and the beginning of something that could be salvaged—if she was willing to face it. The road to redemption would be long. It would be painful. But it would begin with the truth.

For now, Étienne could only hope that the journey toward healing had begun.

12

AFTER THE FALL

Washington, D.C. - Two Weeks Later

Two weeks had passed, and the city of Washington, D.C. was beginning to rebuild itself —piece by piece, block by block. In some ways, it felt like the storm had passed, like the worst of the devastation had been dealt with. Yet, the city still carried the scars of what had happened. The buildings were being repaired, the roads patched up, and the pulse of the nation was slowly returning to something resembling normalcy. But for those who had lived through the aftermath of Katya's machinations, the impact lingered in ways that would take years to fully understand.

The ripple effects of her exposure spread across the entire country. The prison system, a seemingly impervious institution, was now struggling to recover from the chaos she had set into motion with the poisoned food supply. For days, inmates had been dying in the thousands, their deaths a result of a carefully orchestrated plot that had been nearly impossible to trace back to its source. The system had been paralyzed, unable to respond in time to the poison that had run rampant through the nation's jails.

The death toll, initially understated, had spiraled into a tragedy of unprecedented scale. The poison had coursed through the prison system undetected, silently wreaking havoc before authorities could piece together what had happened. By the time they traced the source to Katya, it was already too late. The damage was done, and the public outrage was palpable. The federal government had launched its own investigations, sifting through the wreckage of the crisis, trying to determine how someone so skilled, so elusive, had slipped through the cracks for so long.

But for Étienne, the battle was over.

At least, the physical battle was.

He sat in a small, dimly lit café in the heart of Washington. It was one of those places that never seemed to change, with its old, worn furniture and soft jazz playing quietly in the background. The café, nestled between the remnants of the city's hustle and bustle, felt almost like a sanctuary for Étienne—a place where he could think, where the noise of the world was muffled and the weight of the past few weeks could be temporarily lifted. The hum of traffic outside, distant and muted by the heavy curtains, seemed like a far-off memory as he stared at the worn leather notebook that sat before him.

The notebook was thick with pages, its edges frayed from the many hours he had spent pouring over it. His pen had sketched out every detail of his investigation, of the story he had lived—Katya's rise to power, her delusions, and the catastrophic end of her reign. He had promised to tell her story, and now, with the full weight of everything that had transpired, he was left to decide how much of it the world should know.

Étienne hadn't expected it to feel this way.

He had won. He had neutralized Katya. The threat had been eliminated, the truth revealed. The public was beginning to see the full extent of the monster she had become, and the world was moving on. But despite everything, there was something hollow inside him. A gnawing emptiness that he couldn't quite explain. The destruction she had caused—both in terms of the lives lost and the damage to society—was so vast, so far-reaching, that it felt almost impossible to comprehend. It wasn't just the immediate devastation. It was the ripple effect that would continue for years to come.

The media was still in overdrive. Stories were breaking almost every day, peeling back layers of Katya's twisted world. Investigative reports were being filed, the truth slowly coming to light. Her involvement in various black market networks, her manipulation of the U.S. prison system, her ability to operate under the radar of society's most dangerous corners—it was all being exposed. But despite the media frenzy, despite the sensationalism of her downfall, Étienne knew that no one would ever truly understand the depths of what had driven her. No one would ever fully comprehend how she had become what she was, and why she had been so dangerous. Her legacy, though fractured beyond recognition, would never fully fade. Her name would be etched into history, but the truth of who she really was—how she had become a force of destruction—was far more complicated than anyone would ever realize.

For Étienne, however, this was no longer just a story about a villainous mastermind who had been brought to justice. It had become something much more personal. It was about a woman—one whose actions had left a trail of destruction, but also a woman who had been broken long before she had ever become a threat to anyone else. Katya's tragic backstory, the circumstances that had shaped her madness, the pain she had buried deep inside her—Étienne couldn't shake the feeling that the true story was more about that. It was about how a fractured, damaged person could become so consumed by their own pain that they ended up destroying everything around them.

There had been moments—glimpses, really—when Étienne had seen it in her. The woman she might have been, had life turned out differently. A frightened, desperate girl who had clung to the idea of control because the alternative—facing the chaos of her own feelings—was too unbearable. There had been flashes of vulnerability in her, cracks in the façade she had built so carefully. And for a moment, Étienne had believed there was still a chance for her, that maybe the truth could break through. But that wasn't enough. It wasn't enough to save her.

Étienne sighed and closed the notebook, his hand resting on the cover for a moment. He felt the weight of the decision that lay ahead. Should he release the full details of his investigation—the intimate, painful truths of Katya's rise and fall—or should he bury it all, letting the world forget? Would the world be better off not knowing everything? He knew the public would demand answers, and the media would spin their own narratives to fill the void. But was it really his burden to carry? Was it his place to decide how much of Katya's broken story should be revealed to the world?

It was a question Étienne didn't have an answer to. Not yet.

· · ·

The Final Interview

Étienne sat in the dimly lit room, the weight of the past few weeks pressing down on him like a physical burden. The notebook—the one he had filled with the story of Katya's rise and fall—lay on the table in front of him, its leather cover worn from constant use. It was a story he had lived, breathed, and fought for. But now, as the silence of the room enveloped him, Étienne found himself unable to look at it. The task he had once thought he could handle—the task of telling the world everything about Katya's madness, her destruction, and the lives she had shattered—now seemed like a mountain he could never climb.

A knock at the door broke his reverie. It was a soft, measured knock, not urgent, but persistent. Étienne didn't need to look up to know who it was. He knew Sarah's knock by heart—the gentle, respectful rhythm that marked her presence. After everything they had been through together, her presence in the room felt almost like an anchor in the storm of his thoughts.

"Étienne," she called softly, her voice carrying just above a whisper. "It's time."

He hadn't answered immediately, the words still hanging heavy in his chest, but he finally looked up as Sarah entered. She was the only one who had truly seen the depths of the nightmare, the only one who had walked through the fire with him, from the moment Katya's twisted plan had come to light to the final confrontation that had ended in so much destruction. Her quiet strength, her unshakable presence, had kept him grounded when he feared he might lose himself in the chaos. And now, as the aftermath of everything they had uncovered began to settle, she was the one person who understood the full weight of what he had been through.

She sat down across from him, her eyes soft with empathy but also filled with something deeper—a quiet understanding. Sarah was the kind of person who listened without judgment, who could bear witness to the deepest of burdens without ever flinching. In this moment, Étienne felt that she was the only person left who could share the burden of the truth with him.

"Have you decided?" Sarah asked, her voice gentle but firm, as though she already knew what his answer would be. "About the article. About the story."

Étienne stared at the notebook in front of him, his fingers brushing lightly across the leather surface. He had spent so much time writing, so many hours piecing together every fragment of the investigation, every moment of Katya's descent into madness. It was all there—everything he had uncovered. But now, it felt like a different kind of weight. A weight that wasn't just about justice or truth, but about loss. The innocent lives caught in the crossfire. The destruction she had caused. The devastation that couldn't be undone, no matter how much truth was told.

"No," he said after a long silence. His voice sounded distant, almost hollow. "I can't. I thought I could... but I can't."

The words left his mouth with a finality he hadn't expected. He had been sure—so sure—that once the story was written, once he had the truth on paper, it would be enough. He could give it to the world, and it would bring closure, some semblance of understanding. But now that the moment was here, he realized that closure wasn't what he needed. What he needed was to stop chasing something that could never be fixed.

Sarah nodded, her eyes softening as she listened to him. She understood. She knew exactly what he meant. She could see the exhaustion in his face, the pain behind his eyes—the silent toll that the journey had taken on him. The story the world expected from him was one of victory, of triumph. The narrative was already written, in a way. Katya was defeated, her reign had crumbled, and the world would move on. But Étienne knew that the real story was far more complicated. It was a story about the cost of that victory— the lives lost, the people who would never get their loved ones back, the scars left on everyone involved. The guilt that had become a part of him, woven into his very being, would never fade.

She reached across the table and placed her hand gently over his. Her touch was warm, a subtle but powerful reminder that he wasn't alone in this. "You don't have to be the one to carry the world's weight on your shoulders, Étienne," she said, her voice steady. "Not this time. You've done more than enough."

Étienne looked up at her, his gaze softening. She was right. He had done what he could, and it was more than anyone could have asked of him. He had faced Katya. He had exposed the truth. But there was a part of him, a heavy part, that had believed somehow he could fix everything— if not through action, then through words. The truth would set things right, he had thought. But now, he saw that some things could never be made right. Some damage went too deep.

"I just..." Étienne trailed off, unsure of how to express the heaviness in his heart. "I feel like I've left something unfinished. Something I can't fix. Even with everything we've uncovered, it feels like I'm just running away from it."

Sarah smiled softly, her thumb brushing across the back of his hand as she gave it a gentle squeeze. "You're not running away, Étienne," she reassured him. "You're just... giving yourself permission to stop. You did your part. Now it's time to take care of yourself."

Her words were like a balm to his weary soul. For so long, Étienne had been consumed by the chase, by the need to finish the investigation, to find answers, to bring justice. But Sarah was right. There had to be a point when he stopped. A point when he let go of the weight of the past and started healing—if not for the world, then for himself.

Étienne exhaled deeply, his shoulders relaxing for the first time in weeks. "I just don't know if I can," he admitted, his voice raw with emotion. "I've seen so much. I've carried so much... How do you let go of that?"

Sarah leaned forward, her eyes searching his, understanding the depth of his internal struggle. "You don't let go of it all at once, Étienne. Healing takes time. And it's not about forgetting. It's about learning to live with what you've seen, what you've experienced. You don't have to be strong all the time. You're allowed to be human."

Her words hung in the air like a gentle promise. Étienne didn't know if he was ready to take that step, but for the first time, he felt like it was possible. He wasn't alone in this anymore. He had Sarah by his side—someone who understood, someone who didn't expect him to be a hero, someone who just saw him as Étienne.

And maybe, just maybe, that was enough.

Katya's Fate

Two weeks had passed since Katya's reign of terror had ended, and the world was still reeling from the aftermath of everything she had done. The city was rebuilding itself, the country was picking up the pieces, and yet, somewhere in the midst of all the chaos, Katya's fate remained a bitter question that gnawed at Étienne's soul.

Katya, the woman who had once commanded armies of followers, manipulated systems, and brought nations to their knees, was now confined to a sterile hospital room, a mere shadow of the woman she had been. The woman who had wielded power like a god, who had spun an intricate web of lies and delusions to control everything around her, was no longer capable of forming a coherent thought. Her mind had fractured beyond repair. The poison she had crafted, the horrors she had unleashed, the lives she had ruined—none of it seemed to matter now. In the quiet of her hospital bed, Katya was nothing more than a broken, silent figure.

Her eyes, once cold and calculating, were now vacant, her gaze lost in some distant place. She no longer knew where she was, who she was, or who the people around her were. Her voice—once sharp, commanding, and full of venom—had become an almost inaudible whisper, as if the very essence of her had been drained away. Her hands, which had once held the power to destroy entire systems, now trembled weakly, unable to grasp anything but the cold, sterile air of the room. Katya's delusions had shattered, yes, but the damage to her psyche was permanent. There would be no miraculous recovery, no return to the ruthless mastermind she had once been.

Étienne had visited her only once since her capture. He had been unable to resist—after everything she had done, he had to see her with his own eyes, to witness the end of the woman who had caused so much pain. But when he entered the sterile white room, he found nothing but emptiness staring back at him. Katya's once-proud figure was curled up in a hospital bed, her eyes unfocused, as if she were staring into a void. She didn't acknowledge him. She didn't even seem to know who he was. Her head turned slowly, almost mechanically, in his direction, but there was no recognition, no flicker of the fire that had once burned in her eyes.

For a moment, Étienne stood there, just watching her. There was no anger in his heart, no sense of victory. Only confusion, and something else—something closer to sorrow than anything else. He had expected to see the final act of justice, the moment when she would face the consequences of her crimes. But instead, what he saw was a woman who had been broken by the very forces she had once controlled. The monstrous figure that had haunted his every step was now just a fragile shell, completely undone by her own delusions and the weight of her past.

He had approached her cautiously, unsure of what to say. What could he say to someone like her? To the woman who had destroyed so many lives, who had manipulated and murdered without remorse, who had thought she was invincible? But when he opened his mouth, the words wouldn't come. What could he say to someone who no longer understood anything—who no longer even recognized herself? All that was left was the hollow shell of a woman who had once believed she was a god, now reduced to nothing more than a casualty of her own mind.

Étienne had stayed for a long time, sitting silently by her bedside, watching her drift in and out of a reality only she could understand. Her eyes, dull and unfocused, would occasionally flicker with the faintest hint of recognition— perhaps a momentary glimpse of who she had been, or perhaps just a trick of her shattered mind. He wasn't sure.

Eventually, he had left, the weight of her existence pressing down on him harder than any victory ever could. Katya's fate seemed like a tragic paradox—a woman who had spent her entire life running from her past, from her guilt, from her own humanity, and who had, in the end, destroyed herself in the process. Was it justice? Was it the end she deserved?

Étienne didn't know.

What he knew was that the world would remember Katya as a monster, as the woman who had nearly brought an entire country to its knees. But Étienne had seen her in those final moments, and what he saw wasn't a villain. It was a broken, terrified woman who had been swallowed whole by the lies she had told herself for so long. The guilt, the trauma, the endless weight of the things she had done —it had finally shattered her, and there was no way to undo the damage.

For Étienne, it wasn't a clear-cut victory. The puzzle pieces of her story didn't fit neatly together. Justice had been served in the traditional sense, yes—she had been stopped, her plans unraveled, and her reign of terror ended. But what did it mean to defeat someone who was already defeated by their own mind? What was justice when the person who had committed the atrocities had lost themselves in the process?

In the end, Étienne couldn't reconcile the two opposing truths. He couldn't erase the horror of Katya's actions—her cruelty, her manipulation, her reign of terror. But he also couldn't ignore the woman who had been destroyed by her own fears, her own traumas, and her desperate search for control. He didn't know if she had ever been capable of redemption. What he knew, though, was that Katya had been a victim of her own mind, a victim of a past that had shaped her into something unrecognizable.

Was this what she deserved? Was this what she had wanted all along? Or had it simply been the inevitable consequence of a life lived in denial, a life where the lies she had told herself had finally become too much to bear?

Étienne couldn't answer. Not then, not now.

What he knew, however, was that he could never forget her. The truth of her life—the rise, the fall, the twisted delusions she had clung to—would stay with him forever.

EPILOGUE

New Beginning

The late afternoon sun bathed Washington, D.C., in a warm, golden hue, stretching long shadows across the city. The sky, a deep, fiery orange, seemed to echo the unrest still churning in Étienne's chest. He and Sarah walked together, stepping out of the café that had provided him with some peace after the storm. The world around them was still uncertain, its edges marked by the scars of Katya's actions. Yet there was a shift in the atmosphere—a quiet feeling that things were beginning to calm, that the worst of it had passed.

The sounds of the city continued, but it was a different kind of noise now. The frantic clamor of chaos had softened into something slower, less urgent. People moved through the streets with purpose, but without the same wild energy that had once driven them to fear and frenzy. For the first time in what felt like years, there was room to breathe. Room to think. To start again.

As they walked, Sarah glanced over at Étienne, her expression soft. There was a new kind of quiet between them, one that had been earned through shared hardship. Their journey had been long and painful, but there was an undeniable bond that had formed in the fires of their experiences. Sarah had been with him through the worst of it—the darkest moments when things had seemed impossible, when Katya's reach had felt all-encompassing. She had stood by him when he had lost himself in the fog of the investigation, and had, in many ways, helped him find his way back.

"You know, Étienne," she said, her voice gentle, "I think you've earned the right to move on. You've done your job."

Étienne nodded slowly, but the movement was more reflexive than filled with certainty. He understood what she meant—he had stopped Katya. He had brought an end to her twisted vision and prevented further suffering. He had done what he set out to do, and in many ways, that should have been enough. Yet, there was something inside of him that wouldn't allow him to simply walk away, to simply close the chapter on what had happened and pretend everything was as it had been before.

He turned his gaze toward her, offering a small smile, but it didn't quite reach his eyes. There was a weight there, something deeper. He wasn't ready to let go—not yet.

"Maybe," he said softly, his voice carrying a quiet resolve, "But I think there's still more I can do. I still have a story to write. My story."

Sarah raised an eyebrow, clearly intrigued but also a little surprised. She stopped walking for a moment, her eyes studying him more intently now. "What kind of story?"

Étienne hesitated, looking up at the sky. The sun was setting lower now, the orange glow reflecting off the buildings around them. It felt almost symbolic—like the end of one chapter and the beginning of another. A fresh start, but with all the knowledge and experience that came from what had already happened. He exhaled slowly, as if letting the weight of everything he had carried in silence drift away, even if just for a moment.

"A story of survival," he said, his voice soft but firm. "Not just the people we've lost. But the people who are still here. The ones who are still fighting."

The words hung in the air between them, heavier than he had expected. It was the first time he had allowed himself to articulate it—his own need to find meaning, to find something worth living for after everything had been torn apart. He had seen the devastation Katya had caused, but he had also seen the resilience of the people who had survived. He had witnessed the spark of life that refused to be extinguished, even in the face of unimaginable loss. There was power in survival. In the ability to rebuild, even after everything had seemed destroyed.

As Étienne spoke, he realized that this wasn't just about Katya's downfall, or even about his own personal journey. This was about the world beyond the destruction, the people still left standing after the storm. They were the true story—those who had found ways to continue, to heal, to rise above the pain. The ones who hadn't been defeated, even if they had been scarred.

Sarah nodded thoughtfully, her smile softening as she seemed to grasp the depth of what he was saying. She had seen it too. She had lived it with him—the toll that this investigation had taken, the personal losses, the relentless pursuit of an enemy who had seemed almost unbeatable. But like him, she had also seen something else. Something far more important.

"You're right," she said quietly. "There's still so much left to do. The story's not over yet."

They continued walking together, their footsteps in sync. Étienne's gaze turned once more to the horizon, where the last traces of daylight were fading, leaving behind a cool, twilight blue. The world, much like him, had been through something extraordinary. But it was still moving forward. There was still hope, still room for something new.

In that moment, Étienne realized that maybe the most important part of the story wasn't about what had happened. It wasn't about the wars fought, the villains defeated, or the victories claimed. It was about what would come next. For him. For Sarah. For the world that had been forced to reckon with the darkness Katya had unleashed. There was no going back. There was no undoing the past.

But there was always a new beginning.

And in that new beginning, there was something worth fighting for.

www.ingramcontent.com/pod-product-compliance
Lightning Source LLC
Chambersburg PA
CBHW040907010826
48978CB00013BB/1174